"NEVER FALL FOR THE PREY."

SCARLET

LUNA SAGE BOOK 1

KARI ROBINS

Other Books

The Vörður of Yggdrasil Series
The Rise of the Vörður
The Battle for Yggdrasil - Spring 2023

The Luna Sage Series
Scarlet
Ivory - Fall 2023
Luna - Winter 2023

Magical Midlife Mayhem Series

Almost Tragic Magic- 2024

Table of Contents

A Note from the Author   vi
Into the Forest   2
The Sage   16
Chased   26
Hunter & Prey   34
One Wolf, One Hunter, One Room   42
Fighting Ghosts   52
Awaken   62
The Harvest Festival   70
Alone in the Woods   90
Shooting Lessons   100
A Peak into the Past   108
The Hunt   114
The Wolf   122
Wild Wolfe   132
Back to the Woods   138
We Go   138
Killer Wolf   146
Brothels, Bar Fights, & Bars   154
Over the River   164
And through the   170
Woods   170
Enlisting Help   176
A Huntin' We   184
 Will Go   184
McGowan   194
Luna Sage   202
Acceptance   212
Mated   218
Afterword   234
Acknowledgments   236

A Note from the Author

This story is the darkest thing I've ever written. I, personally, have no triggers, and writing this made me cry several times. This story is a dark werewolf novel, so humans will be mixed in with the wolves. This is a trilogy that gets progressively darker. The first book isn't as dark as the rest, but I don't want anyone to get hooked on this story without knowing what you're signing up for. Here's a list for each books triggers:

Scarlet
Luna Sage Book 1

- There is only one full on sex scene but lots of play. Because of the fantasy nature of the story and the plot of the bad guy, my characters do not practice safe sex either.
- Some consensual blood play.
- My MC's are hunters in both human and wolf form, so some fictitious animals will be harmed.
- There will be an abundance of violence (mostly wolf on wolf) and blood.
- Scarlet ends on a Happily For Now

Ivory
Luna Sage Book 1

- Sex, sex, and more sex… some consensual, some dub-con, and some non-con. Because of the fantasy nature of the story and the plot of the bad guy, my characters do not practice safe sex either.
- Some consensual and non-consensual blood play.
- Bad things will happen to both of my MC's. There

will be torture, forced drug use, and will be forced to harm innocent humans.

- Non-con between humans and wolves. (In human form.
- There will be an abundance of violence (mostly wolf on wolf) and blood.
- There will be some scenes that some might consider cheating, but it is all caused by a drug or Magic.
- Ivory ends on a "Everything is fucked" cliffhanger.

<u>Luna</u>
Luna Sage Book 3

- Sex, sex, and more sex... some consensual, some dub-con, and some non-con. Because of the fantasy nature of the story and the plot of the bad guy, my characters do not practice safe sex either.
- Some consensual and non-consensual blood play.
- Bad things will happen to both of my MC's. There will be torture, forced drug use, and will be forced to harm innocent humans.
- Non-con between human's and wolves. (In human form.
- There will be an abundance of violence (mostly wolf on wolf) and blood.
- There will be some scenes that some might consider cheating, but it is all caused by a drug or Magic.
- Final book ends on a Happily Ever After.
-

Playlist

I love writing to music. I created a playlist of songs that I felt my main character Scarlet would listen to if she lived our world.

To all the women who grew up
listening to fairy tales wishing her
prince charming would come save her.

Save him instead.

1
Into the Forest
Scarlet

The early morning breeze washed over me in icy waves. Each gust of wind poured the scent of the forest into my soul. I gritted my teeth, already aching to be out hunting.

My mother and father had not even bothered to show up at my house to say their goodbyes this morning. Mother hardly spoke to me these days; she made her opinion on my profession clear long ago. Both mother and father had accepted that I was already dead, so why bother?

I paced anxiously near the edge of my hometown, Whitehaven, waiting for the others to drag out their farewells. The weight of the familiar wooden crossbow strapped to my back calmed me. Walking over to the one creature that hadn't let me down in the past ten winters, I checked the saddle strapped to Jericho, my black gelding. I pushed aside the image of his previous owner as I scratched behind his ear. Thinking of the past would only get me killed.

The commander of the Huntsman watched over us as we waited to be released into the Wild Woods that surrounded the kingdom of Breton. His signal would begin our season of killing.

In the early days, humans were hunted to near extinction. We named our cold season the 'Blood Season' for all the lives that were lost to wolf attacks. Once the snow stuck to the ground, it wasn't long before the blanket of white along the forest floor was stained with blood. I knew from my many winters of experience that at least half of these men either wouldn't return or would return maimed.

Shaking myself from my musings, I mounted Jericho. Men had finally parted from their wives and lovers and gathered near the forest's edge.

More horses joined alongside Jericho, though the men riding them tried their best to ignore my presence. Most of the men stood a full head and shoulders above me, and more than a few were twice as wide. My small stature didn't stop me from out-hunting them every season.

All the steely gazes of the wives huddled behind us bore into my back. The women thought I rode off into the woods to screw their husbands, and the men thought I hunted to steal their glory.

It didn't matter that I had set the bar for the past ten winters for the highest kills per season. I was a *woman*. Despite my skills, my presence was unwelcome. *A woman succeeding? Perish the thought.*

I tried to ignore the sobs from the women my fellow Huntsmen were leaving behind. I held my face as still as stone. I wanted to hunt. I needed to hunt.

The woods called to me like a siren's song. Out there, amid the brambles and branches, was my happiness. I could be me. No one would watch me. No one would judge me. I could be who I had been born to be.

I longed to have the coarse, brittle bark cut into my palms while I looked down on my prey from the trees above. The breeze shifted toward the forest, beckoning me to join. I could already sense the comforting pressure of my thighs resting on the thick branches. My small build made me agile. All the winters of climbing the trees had prepared me for gaining the high ground over both wolves and Hunters.

Only after the last of the women were dragged away from their men did the commander stand in front of us to give his annual speech.

"They were once human, but lycanthropy spreads through the body like a disease. All humanity is lost, and they are forever locked into the monstrous beasts. That is why we hunt them every year, and one day very soon, we will be rid of them all.

"They are always deadly, but even more so as the moon grows full. The younger ones have less control over their beast, while older ones can sometimes hide their true nature. Do not be fooled. No matter how docile they seem, the only wolf who won't attack you is a dead wolf."

I sighed. I had lost count of how many times I had heard him give the same prattling speech. I could give it for him at this point. After my first hunt he had said I was one of them and that I'd be protected. I scoffed at my own memories. He was just like every other man not following through on his promises.

"They aren't immortal, but lycanthropy slows aging down significantly. There are rumors of an ancient wolf that is over five hundred winters old. The older they are, the more cunning they become. The wolves may be hard to kill, but they aren't invincible."

A few of the older men around me gave a knowing laugh at the commander's words.

"You cannot use holy water or crosses to kill or ward them off. That's for vampires—at least according to the legends. The best way to kill them is to use quicksilver. Any form of silver, really."

I watched as the commander handed one of the young Hunters a silver-tipped arrow. The practice was a bit antiquated, in my opinion. Many winters ago, I had replaced the silver-tipped arrows with quicksilver bolts. I made the inside of each bolt with a solid quicksilver shaft, and on the outside, the hollowed-out ash shaft helped the bolt to splinter the flesh. For my arrowheads, I used broadheads made entirely of silver." One-shot, one-kill was my motto.

The commander clapped a few of the younger boys on the back one last time before releasing us all for the hunt.

"Be faster. Be quicker. Be deadlier. Good luck, men."

The men on foot spread out in all directions, setting up a perimeter around Whitehaven. Those on horseback branched out on the narrow trails they made every year, heading for spots deeper into the forest.

But I rode south where I knew the older and wiser wolves would head.

The lands between the villages were thick with trees, as we only cleared what we needed. We had one large field outside the village for our grains, but each home had a small garden in the yard responsible for feeding the family. Chickens and goats roamed the street within the protection of the walls.

Whitehaven was lucky enough to have an alternating angled palisade wall surrounding most of the village. Its sharp pointed tops deterred most wolves from jumping it, but now and then, one would be brave enough to try. Most villages couldn't afford that luxury and relied on the Huntsmen to protect them. I was heading toward one such village.

The narrow path to Silverbarrow threaded through the timber like a seamstress' thread through the eye of a needle. Each turn was tightly woven into another. It was all too easy to get lost.

The trees, while beautiful and tranquil, served as an abundant cover for the werewolves. Luckily for me, the telltale signs to watch for while tracking prey came second nature to me now.

With Jericho, I could travel much farther than most of the others. He was as seasoned as I was and would not be as distracted as the younger ponies were. Jericho had been with me on hunts so often that he would no longer bolt at the first sign of a wolf. Instead, he was like a partner.

The last time I ignored the horse had cost me dearly, so I learned to listen to his warnings. Flicking his tail faster, shaking his head, or snorting meant a predator was nearby. He was my early warning sign. Too bad the best hunting grounds were impenetrable by horseback.

All my senses were on high alert. I stayed strictly on my path. Many of the other Huntsmen traveled in pairs, but after my own naivete on that first hunt I had learned solitude was best. The sound of someone's heavy breathing or the snapping of a twig at the wrong time could cost me my life.

A sound in the distance snapped me back to attention. The odd sensation of being watched reminded me to be alert. Goosebumps ran down my arms as my eyes scanned the forest.

Jericho and I made it to the outskirts of the tiny village without a single sighting of the wolves. The road narrowed the closer we got to Silverbarrow. We paused to pay respect to a small group of mourners surrounding three fresh earth mounds in a graveyard much too large for a town so small.

We passed two large posts with rusty metal hanging off the side where massive doors once stood. People walked past us, jumping over deep ruts and blood stained roads, not bothering to look up at us. Those that did see our red cape nodded slightly before running off in the opposite directions they'd been heading. My heart raced as the villagers fled.

Doors slammed and locked behind us as we trotted further into the village. We continued on, ignoring the reactions from the villagers and headed toward the inn in the center of town. It was the only public building with a stable. I had been here once before, but it had been many winters. Nothing really changed. A half a dozen shops stood in the center of town. Each building was being held together with bailing twine and looked as if they were on their last string.

I hitched Jericho to a wooden post and pushed through the door. Dust coated every surface, tickling my nose, which I crinkled to keep from sneezing. A petite girl stood at the counter, shifting through keys. She jolted as I stepped up to her.

"I need to stable my horse." I looked at the innkeeper. Her hands shook, and she dropped the keys she was holding. "Where's the old man?" I asked her.

"He... he... died." She backed away as she spoke. "Wolves."

"I'm sorry." I tried to show sympathy, but people die every day. That is why I do what I do. "My horse?"

"How long for?" the small girl asked. She wrung her hands on her filthy dress, not stepping closer.

"Not sure. All depends on the hunt."

Her eyes grew wide as she finally took me in. "S-Scarlet?" she breathed out.

Suppressing a sigh, I nodded. I could only imagine what this girl had heard about me. At first glance, I didn't look like a Hunter. But my calloused hands, chapped face, and muscular build could only account for a few things. The crossbow still attached to my back was a dead giveaway. But mostly the rumors that spread like wildfire about the lone female Huntsman followed me everywhere I went.

"V-very well, ma'am," the innkeeper stuttered.

"Here's some coin to care for him."

"Thank you. Bring him around back, and the stable boy will take him for you."

Nodding, I walked out the door.

I brought Jericho around to the stables, handing the reins off to the short but stout boy. His eyes roamed over my red cloak and hands shook slightly as he took the reins from me.

"Let me just grab my things, and I'll be off." I grabbed my pack and quiver and walked around to the front of him. "If you keep him safe, there will be extra coin in it for you." The boy's grimace turned to a grin at my words, and he nodded at me.

Rubbing the horse's nose, I thought about everything Jericho and I had been through. Leaving him behind tore at my heart.

"Now you behave, Jericho. I'll be back soon." The smell of fresh meat wafted in the air, making my stomach grumble and reminding me that I needed to stock up before heading out. "Is that the butcher shop?" I asked the stable boy.

"Yes, ma'am. Just next door."

"Thanks. You take good care of him. Okay?" He nodded as I gave him one last look. Content that Jericho would be fine until my return, I walked off toward the butcher.

The small shop glistened with the polished-wood floors. The storefront held a few glass cases filled with meat. Behind the long metal counter stood a wall with a giant window that peered into the cutting room. Sharp metal hooks dangled from the ceiling as they waited for carcasses gathered by local farmers.

"Can I help you, Miss?" A kindly older woman stood behind the large counter. The woman was no taller than me yet at least twice as wide. She wore a clean black apron, and her hair was tied tight to her head in a bun.

I stepped closer as I spoke, "Yes, ma'am. You have any smoked meats for sale?"

She eyed my pack and bow before replying. "You a Hunter? Don't get many of y'all 'round here."

"Yes, ma'am."

"Never a female, neither." She threw the worn and bloody rag she had been using to wipe her hands on the counter.

"No, ma'am. Not many women are brave enough to do what I do."

"Or foolish. Why do it?"

"I have my reasons, ma'am." A long-buried memory threatened to surface, a young girl with a wide smile playing with me near the edge of the forest.

Pushing the memory down, I looked back at the woman. "The smoked meats?" I tried to hide the annoyance in my voice.

"Ah yes. We do that, Miss. You want something in particular? Or just anything to take with you in the forest, I'spect?" She raised a brow at me.

"Yes, ma'am. Anything would be fine."

"We gots some venison sausage and loads of jerky. We even have some without spices, so it shouldn't have much of a scent."

"I'll take a little of each, please."

"All right, Miss. I'll pack some up for ya." She hobbled off toward the back room. Digging out a few more coins, I waited as patiently as I could for the woman to return.

She emerged from the backroom with several packages in her hands a moment later. "You sure you really want to keep going out there with them wolves? They're wretched creatures. They've killed so many strong men, and you're just a g—."

"Yes, ma'am. Have been doing this going on ten winters now. No point stopping now." I interrupted her before she could say something she'd regret.

She raised an eyebrow, looking mildly impressed as she handed me the packages of meat. "Well, just see you don't die out there—and keep killing as many of those bastards as you can, Scarlet." She took my coins without another word and walked away.

I was used to people, women especially, trying to talk me out of being a Huntsman, but it got annoying. If I didn't know what I was doing, the Huntsmen would not have allowed me to go out.

I left the butcher shop, and the cold wind chilled my skin. My mood had grown foul. I hated to linger in villages longer than was absolutely necessary. No matter how big or how small, they all held nosey people.

I tucked the meat deep in my pack as I walked. Though I couldn't smell the food through all the wrapping, I didn't want to take a chance that a wolf might.

I headed out of the village, pulling the hood of my cloak over my head, and walked toward the tree line.

Once outside the village, I followed a small, man-made path into the forest until I picked up a narrow game trail. I knew the thin path other animals traveled would take me deeper into the forest. Although it was mid-day, the canopy overhead blocked out most of the light.

Tonight would be a moonless sky. I might as well get used to the darkness now. The colder season was upon us. Grass held onto the last bit of life it could. Leaves had already fallen, leaving a crunchy bed for me to walk on.

For most Hunters, the crunch of the underbrush might be a death sentence. But I was small, which meant lighter footsteps.

The trees grew in age and girth the further in I traveled. Normally, I would find the largest tree and camp out in the branches, but it was getting late. I would need to find shelter before night fell and the wolves descended.

Far ahead on the edge of the horizon, I spotted a massive tree with branches thicker than my waist just as the sun's final rays peeked through the branches.

I picked up my pace, quickly reaching my destination. I pulled off my quiver to retrieve my special arrow with the blunt tip on the front end and a rope tied to the other. Cocking my crossbow, I placed the bolt into its slot and aimed high in the tree. I fired my arrow, and it wrapped neatly around the largest branch.

I gave the rope a quick tug before I strapped my quiver and bow back over my shoulder. Using the rope and the tree trunk, I climbed up to the wide branch.

I quickly unraveled the rope, swinging it under the branch beneath me and strapping myself in. This position wasn't the most comfortable, but with the small blanket I pulled from my bag, I could sleep safely away from any predators.

My mind drifted back to my first hunt. The softness of the black and red blanket contrasted with his hard body on top of me. We were supposed to be hunting but his lips brushed against mine and I ignored my instincts. The fresh blood and his weight pinning me to the ground finally broke my trance. Rage fueled those first kills. I couldn't find the wolf that had killed my best friend or my lover, but still the blood of those first two wolves quenched the fire, if only for a short time.

It was quiet and peaceful alone in a tree. I spent several winters learning how to climb and sleep on the thick branches. Back then I didn't have the strength I do now. I had spent many sleepless nights in the duff with one eye constantly scanning the forest for the unseen.

I shook those old fears from my mind. They would only keep me awake. I settled in for the night with my crossbow firmly gripped in my arms. Sleep came fleetingly that night. Every snap, every gust of wind, made me jump. This hunting season was going to be long.

2
The Sage
Conri

I held the packs together as long as I could. I wasn't just their alpha. I was the alphas' alpha; I was their Sage. But I no longer could lead them. I was only a liability to them.

The wolves spread wide, and each pack roamed their territory until it was time to head back north to our home, Madadh-Allaidh. We needed to hunt and to feed, but the violence within the packs had grown wild as they began killing for sport. In my three hundred winters, I had seen far too much death. I already had too much blood on my hands, and I needed to leave before karma caught up with me.

Sneaking out in the middle of the night was a cowardly thing to do, but there were enough members of the pack I had been running with that would kill me if they found me deserting. This way was better. They would wake in the morning, but I would already be long gone.

Pussy. Wolfe's voice echoed in my head. I knew he wanted us to stay and fight but I had to leave.

I gathered the rest of my things into my pack and threw it over my broad shoulders. I took far too much from our people already to take anything else. I would have to find food elsewhere.

Firelight guided my way through the sleeping men and women sprawled over the cave floor. I stepped around them, leaving the sound of their snores behind as I walked out into the cool night air. I let out a sigh of relief.

I paused, waiting for my eyes to adjust to the dark, moonless sky. Leaving tonight when the moon was at its calmest would keep all but the wildest of the pack from following me.

The night was calm as I walked deeper into the trees. My hot breath lingered in the air. A twig snapped behind me, but before I could turn to look, I slammed hard into something in front of me, nearly stumbling backward.

"You think you can just run from us?" a voice in the dark snapped. The monster within me, Wolfe, growled to be released and destroy these wolves.

"You have been growing weaker." Another familiar voice sneered from behind me.

"And you know what happens to the weak ones in the pack...," the first voice said.

"They get culled." Two more voices from behind me sang out together.

It had to be the twins. Wolfe's eyes found them in the darkness. They stood tall and gangly. Their blond, stringy hair draped over their shoulders. Olivia clung to her brother in a scrap of cloth that barely covered her tits and shorts that showed her ass cheeks. Oliver's fingers wrapped around her middle, making my stomach turn. He wore black jeans that were undone and hanging low on his hip.

Oliver and Olivia skirted the line of sanity. No one ever spoke of what they did in the shadows. Most leaders would have dealt with them long ago, but twins are so rare among our kind, I believed they were special. And now that Oliver was alpha, killing him would be suicide. The mistake of letting them live long ago might cost me my life tonight.

I barreled past the figures in front of me. I could at least outrun them.

"You really think we are going to let you just leave?" Oliver called after me.

"We will make it quick, but only if you stay." His sister's honeyed words pierced right through me, making me queasy. Our packs included few females among us, and she was the prime example of why. Insanely jealous, she had cut down a few of her own pack mates simply for looking at her brother. I could face an army of wolves like Oliver—but it took only one of her to send chills down my spine.

I ran as fast as I could to gain some distance from the rest of the pack. Five I could handle. Forty would be a problem. Branches snapped as the four of them charged after me.

I used to love the thrill of the hunt, but now that I was the hunted…

Sweat rolled down my face as I quickened my pace. I had to find a clearing. The trees were too thick here to do what needed to be done. Fast as I might be on two feet, I needed to shift. My eyes, fully functioning now, darted from side to side. Finally finding what I needed, I changed direction. The small, grassy knoll was just big enough for me.

I knelt in the grass, stripping off my clothes and shoes. I quickly stuffed them in my pack. Crouching on all fours, I summoned the curse within me.

Pain seared through me as my arms and legs twisted at odd angles. I slammed my jaw shut tight to keep from giving away my position as fur sprouted all over my body. Every muscle burned as they mutated into him.

I despised Wolfe for every pain he had caused me, but I knew he would save me now.

We were the fastest on four paws throughout all the packs that roamed Breton. We could, and would, outrun every wolf—except for our own.

We ran until their distant howls grew faint and silenced altogether.

Pathetic pussy. Why didn't you let me kill them all? Wolfe growled at me.

I tried to ignore him as we ran through the darkness.

We ran all night, and when the sun rose, we kept running. Only when the sun was setting again and every muscle in our body was aching did we finally slow down, taking in our surroundings.

We had been running blindly, trying to get out of Oliver's territory as fast as possible. We might have been the Sage and ruled over the other alphas, but by leaving we had forfeited our reign and life if they caught up with us. We scanned from side to side, trying to find something, but no mountains or rock formations looked familiar to us. Sniffing the air didn't help us either. We were completely and utterly lost.

We walked around for several minutes, trying to find some landmark to tell us whose territory we were in now. Other packs would not take kindly to an alpha walking into their territory uninvited, even though I was their Sage still as far as they knew. Some would rip our throats out. Others would tear us to shreds and then eat our bloody carcass for dinner. News of my desertion would travel fast. We needed to be careful.

Snow had begun to fall, which was just another stark reminder of the danger we were constantly in. It was hunting season. If the twins didn't get us, the Hunters would. We had to find cover before one of those trigger-happy fools shot us.

The Huntsmen were spiteful men. The scar on our back proved that they hated all wolves without fail. And in our wolf form, we were hard to miss.

Even in the darkness, we stood out. With the sun shining down on our damp fur, we glistened like a beacon, which was why wolves mostly hunted at night.

No amount of brush would totally obscure our form. We were the largest wolf in all the packs. We outweighed our prehistoric brother, the dire wolf, by at least seven stones and could have easily looked down at him. Not to mention, a gigantic wolf carrying a pack on its back would certainly arouse suspicion.

Our dark fur, at least, would hide us from any Hunters that might lie in wait in the distance. We sniffed the cold ground for any trace of humans or wolves but found only the familiar smells of the forest. A rabbit had passed by recently. Squirrels darted across the ground before scampering up the nearby trees. Once we were certain no threat was nearby, we stalked through the underbrush in search of shelter.

We didn't have to search long before finding a small cave. Wolfe was a fierce predator to even a large bison, so we charged in without fear. If any animals were hiding in here, they would be in for a terrible surprise.

Mercifully, a quick search of our new home proved it was vacant. Our body and mind couldn't take much more walking. We needed to rest.

The cool rocks soothed our sore feet as we curled up against the wall. Wolves always ran at a much higher temperature than other animals, and we had been running all night and day. The icy rocks beneath us were a welcome reprieve.

Our eyes were heavy as we settled in. We didn't have the energy to shift back into human form. Besides, we wanted to be ready for anything that might stumble in while we slept. Only a fool would wake the monster asleep in the darkness.

Wolfe

100 winters ago on a full moon night.

I have been tracking the animal that killed our love for nearly six months now. Finally, catching up to him sends waves of adrenaline through me. Conri isn't much for the hunt these days, but I'm salivating at the thought of sinking my teeth and claws into my prey.

I dig at the soft ground with my paws as fresh scents fill my nose. I sniff him out. He is close. Every muscle tenses at a sound in the distance.

My ears twitch from side to side, trying to pinpoint where he is. He has evaded us long enough. It is high time he faces pack justice. Conri will disapprove of my methods. But then again, he isn't here to make that decision.

He's never fully accepted me. He fights our nature at every step, but we are wolves and that means we are cold-blooded killers.

I don't enjoy the hunt. I live for it. He will only hunt when he is hungry.

Pussy.

I hunted for sport, for the rush of blood pumping faster and faster through my veins, and for the wind lashing at our fur as we ran. But mostly for the coppery tang of first blood on our tongue.

I froze in the cool night air when I found him. He would try and run, but that doesn't matter. I was faster.

Digging my paws into the earth, I launched myself straight for his path. He hears me crashing through the trees and darts past me, hurtling in the opposite direction.

Skidding to a halt, I turn on my back paws and sprint after him. Branches whip at my face, but I continue to run. His fear permeates the air with its putrid stench. My muscles burn as I push myself faster.

His silhouette comes into view. He is a much smaller wolf than I. A growl from deep within me comes spilling between my teeth. Memories of our love's mangled body sends boiling rage throughout my entire being. I want nothing more than to see his body treated the same.

Nipping at his heels, I plunge my fangs in. I bite down hard into the soft flesh of his thigh. He howls in pain but keeps running. My jaws lock on tight to my prey. I am not about to let him live… not after her.

Finally, he collapses into the mud.

Releasing his injured leg, I walk to where his head lay against the earth.

You thought you could get away with killing her? I project my words to his mind.

I…I didn't…. Even in my head, I can hear the pleading in his voice. I didn't kill her. I swear.

Every criminal says they are innocent. What makes you any different? I can smell her all over him even now. There is no doubt in my mind I have my man.

I lick the bitter blood from my muzzle as I pace around him.

I swear. I don't know who did, but it wasn't me. His shrill whimper floats through the air around us. Conri, please.

Oh, there is no Conri. Only Wolfe is here tonight. Isn't that fun for you?

I lean down to where he is cowering in the mud and snap at his ear. Crimson blood spills down his muzzle.

He tries to squirm away from me, tucking his long tail underneath him. Despite his show of submission, I will not relent. I wrap my jaws around the scruff of his neck, throwing him to his side.

I do so love to play with my food. Please, try to run.

His body shakes beneath me as I step toward him. He inches away, but I pounce, pinning him in place. Desperate whines seep out of him as I bite down on his neck. I don't release him until a river of blood pools at my paws.

Was she as scared as you are right now? I think not, though. My love was a lot fiercer than you. So how did you kill her? You must have tricked her. It's the only way a coward like you could have bested someone like her.

He squirms underneath me. His eyes are wide with terror. Fury rises within me. I wonder if my love had looked the same when he killed her.

I swear to you. It wasn't me.

Enough lies. Quick as a viper, I sink my fangs into his throat. His body finally goes still. I don't look back as I walk away.

We woke up shivering at the memories of that night. It had been many winters since Wolfe took control like that, though he would deny it if pressed. I knew he thought that night was the moment I started to lose faith in us and our ability to lead.

The sun was beginning to rise, peaking through the cave's entrance. We tried to stand. We needed to keep running, but our exhaustion was too great. We would never make it like this. Curling back up, we pushed away the memories and drifted off to sleep again.

3
Chased
Conri

The pain of fangs sinking deep into our back paw woke us. Our face scraped across the sharp rocks as we struggled to stand. Wolfe tried to kick at the beast that held us, but our efforts were useless. We could not find the power to throw him off.

The midday sun temporarily blinded us as he released our leg. We limped to a stand to face our captors. The twin wolves stood side by side. Mud and burs caked their yellow fur from their night run. Oliver growled at us while his sister took a playful nip at him.

If only you would have mated with me, Conri. Olivia's menacing voice echoed in my head.

She stepped up to us and attempted to nuzzle against our dark fur, but Wolfe snapped our jaws at her. Oliver lunged for our throat and pinned us to the ground before we could take a breath.

Try that again, and it will be your instant death. He ordered us to drag you back to Madadh-Allaidh to face justice. I would hate for you to miss the trials.

Oliver's jowls pulled back into a menacing sneer. He would enjoy watching us go through hell for our crimes. Even Wolfe shook with fear at the thought of the trials. A millennium had passed since someone survived the tests.

The scents of other wolves filled the air, and we knew we were surrounded. A wide mouth snapped at our heels, forcing us forward. I growled at the wolf behind us, warning them to watch their teeth as I bared my own.

The twins turned their backs to us—a sure sign they didn't believe us a threat. They trotted off the way they had come, but their hackles still stood on end. The other wolves were getting impatient with our unwillingness to comply. One bit down hard on our tail. We whipped around, swiping at the other wolf with our long claws and lunging for the wolf's neck.

The one who bit us went down first. He whimpered as Wolfe's fangs found his throat. We increased the pressure in our jaw until the traitor's blood sprayed into our mouth and his legs stilled beneath us. Guilt over killing a member of the pack never came.

The smaller one beside him howled in agony. His hackles raised as we crept toward him. We lunged for him, but before we could reach him, more wolves latched onto our back.

We yowled in anguish as the rest joined in the attack. We needed to escape. Our body went limp as panic overcame us. Dozens of bite wounds littered our fur.

They had orders to keep us alive until we reached Madadh-Allaidh, but they could still injure us. The blood in the dirt belonged to us as much as our captors. We had no way to fight off the wolves that still clutched to our fur, let alone the others surrounding us. One way or another, we would have to pay for the blood on our teeth.

Our hackles lowered, and our growl stopped. The other wolves around us immediately accepted our submission. We surrendered, if only to live to fight another day.

We walked until the moon hung high in the sky. Our captors were bedding down for the night when Wolfe's keen ears heard something the others hadn't. We heard our sisters pack surround us.

Focusing our hearing, we heard them approach. Our wolves—the ones still loyal to us—now surrounded the temporary den. The morons that took us didn't notice as our allies closed in.

We let loose a small growl of approval. Then Kelly stepped into the makeshift camp, and we rose to meet her.

At my movement, the twins lifted their muzzles. Their noses sniffed the air. Both of their heads snapped to attention, and the rest of our enemies stilled when they saw her and the rest of our rescuers.

A deep rumble escaped our throat, and the wolves who captured us cowered. They were willing to take us on alone. They were not willing to risk an all-out attack.

We are leaving now, or we will feast on your blood and bones, Wolfe snarled at them. Pulling at the magic within us, we begged the gods that we still had some control over them. We commanded them to stay through the mental bond and to our surprise the wolves froze at the order but our control was weak, and they'd soon break free.

All wolves know to never turn your back to your enemies, but we would never cower to lesser wolves. My sister's pack exited the clearing first. Our piercing gaze met Olivia's. She would not submit with the rest of them.

Stay away, we commanded Olivia, before turning our back to her.

Olivia foolishly charged at us, even though she knew she would never be faster than Wolfe. Our jaws met her throat before she knew what hit her.

Let me snap this pretty little bitch's neck in two. I'll make it quick.

Wolfe had grown tired of her idiocy.

No, I growled. Reluctantly, he released her, letting her limp back to her brother.

This time, we kept our eyes on Olivia as we moved. We walked out, facing her as she made to block our path. With one last warning-growl, we walked past Olivia. She snarled the entire time, even as we disappeared between the trees.

We kept on high alert listening for any sounds of pursuit until we found my sister and her pack.

They will find us eventually. Someone ordered my trial, we informed them. *How many are with you?*

The six of us are all that remains. My sister's head bowed low in shame. *Amarok took control of the alpha's the moment you left.*

Amarok! That bastard. He's been trying to take my seat for several winters but too afraid to challenge me. How can he just take the seat? There are rules we must all abide by.

He is a coward, but he is strong and slightly psycho. Everyone was too afraid to fight his control. But we, she nodded to the rest of her pack, *ran the moment we knew you were gone.*

Stepping closer, we brushed the side of her face with our muzzle.

Thank you, Kelly. What would we do without our little sister?

Pulling away, we spoke to the rest. *But you should go back. We cannot have your deaths on our heads as well.*

Like hell! Our sister barked back. But before we could respond, the howls from behind us said they had broken free of the command.

Run!

We shouted to the others as we led the way through the trees. The sounds of our pursuers urged us forward. Fighting Wolfe's control, we continued to run.

I just wanted to live my life out in peace. *Why was Amarok bothering with an old wolf like us?*

We were faster than even my sister, who was half our size, but still she was at my heels. We escaped our enemy, but they weren't far behind.

We need to hide. We can't outrun all of them, she said breathlessly.

We scanned the horizon. Our ears heard the water first. Even in the darkness of the night, Wolfe's eyes quickly found the river to our left.

Shifting our path, we headed straight for water. Without a second thought, we leapt for the bank on the other side. Our paws slammed back into the mud with a squelch.

We turned back to where Kelly stood on the other side of the creek. Our sister meant the world to us—even if

Wolfe would never admit it. We couldn't let her get hurt for our mistakes.

Go! She spoke firmly. *We will give you time! You are my brother, and my Sage. I will protect you.*

No! We threw all our command into the word. We didn't know why we thought she would listen to us now.

Don't worry, brother. They aren't stronger than me and my pack. Now, go! She yelled again.

Several moon rises had passed since I left Kelly on that riverbank, but the sounds of her howling still echoed in my nightmares. I could not get her look of fierce determination out of our head. She and her wolves had protected us. Kelly would never forgive me if I risked death trying to find them. I simply wanted to be left alone, but Wolfe would fight to his last breath.

Distant howls broke me from my trance. I didn't recognize the howls, and no one reached out through the mental tether. I couldn't be sure if the howl belonged to friend or foe.

We couldn't go back. The trials would kill us.

You're a coward. Wolfe's furious words echoed in my mind, and I struggled to maintain control.

Branches and underbrush smacked my face and snagged our fur, but we kept running. We could smell the village up ahead. If we changed, we could hide among the humans.

A lone doe crossed in front of us, and our stomach rumbled in response.

We needed to eat.

Our pack moved around this time of year to find the best game. Deer roamed the fields in early fall, but by the time snow coated the ground, we would have to seek more elusive prey like the big cats that hid high on the mountains.

We glanced around again at the unfamiliar territory. I struggled to decide which would be worse, allowing ourselves to be tracked as a wolf or becoming nearly defenseless as a human?

We dug our paws into the dirt and braced for the pain we knew would come. Our fur retracted, leaving our flesh raw. Joints twisted back to my human form, and our claws receded. I shook off the contortion of Wolfe's face, completing the transformation.

I hadn't noticed the rain on my fur, but the icy drops coming down in sheets froze my sensitive skin. I shrugged off the tattered remains of the bag. The clothes were bloody but mostly intact, so I dressed quickly. If I was fast enough, they wouldn't know where I went.

A rustle from behind startled me as I threw my shirt over my head. The sound reached my ears moments before the bolt pierced the flesh at my back.

I grunted as the force slammed me into the earth. The coppery scent of fresh blood invaded my nose as heat rushed through my body.

"Silver!" I spat bile onto the forest floor. Staggering to my feet, I tried to look over my shoulder. The arrow protruded just under my right shoulder blade. I reached, but strained to grab it. Twisting my right arm around my back, I yanked the wooden shaft out.

I fell against the tree nearest me and grunted through a clenched jaw. The ash wood burned my palms, but the bolt was out. I slumped to the ground. The broadhead had come loose and was still stuck deep in my skin. I gasped for air.

I hadn't smelled or sensed a human in weeks. No one other than the Huntsmen used silver arrows. Unless... My heart froze.

"The Silver Silence," I whispered to myself. I scanned the forest through blurry eyes trying to find them. The Silver Silence were creatures that came from an unknown place but had served the wolves for centuries. They were impossible to track—even by the strongest wolf. I should have known Amarok would have called them, the one creature the wolves would trust to take down a rogue. And this one was after me now.

Adrenaline forced me to my feet. I stumbled forward in search of anything to defend myself. I listened intently as the other wolves slowed, but their steps ceased abruptly.

I sniffed the air, and I immediately knew why. The smell of lavender floated through the air, mixed with an undeniably female scent.

They were afraid of her. Even The Silver Silence wouldn't come this close to a Hunter. I couldn't sense much else from the female, but I knew I had to get to her.

I needed help, and I had to risk exposing myself to a human in order to survive. I dragged my feet toward her scent as fast as my weakened body would let me.

4
Hunter & Prey
Scarlet

I wrapped my crimson cloak tighter around my body to brace the oncoming wind, which forced me to shift my stance in the tree. The cold never bothered me, but the wind nearly blew me from my perch. It had only been seven moonrises since I left my village, and I hadn't found any signs of wolves.

My bones ached from sitting in the tree for so long. Each year, we had fewer and fewer wolves to hunt. The townspeople rejoiced to hear this news, but soon I would be left without a job when the wolves became extinct.

I had known little else than this life. I wouldn't know what to do with myself without the hunt.

The first quarter-moon hung high in the sky, meaning the full moon would soon create chaos throughout the forest.

The icy rain forced me to abandon my hiding nest. Normally I'd sleep in the forest–I was more at home in the trees than in my own bed–but I couldn't risk a fire.

Packing up my things, I would head back into town and get a room at the inn where I'd left Jericho.

My foot slipped on the wet bark as I descended the tree, sending me slamming into the earth. A deep cough echoed my breathing. I froze. How had I not heard or sensed another person so close to me?

More coughs filled the quiet around me as they got closer. Quickly, I removed myself from the ground and ducked behind the tree from which I had fallen.

"Shit," I breathed out.

My crossbow and quiver lay just out of reach, and the silhouette of a man approached then fell to the forest floor. I reached for the knife in my boot and waited to see if this stranger would be friend or foe.

Conri

Searing pain burned through my body. I had to keep moving. If they found me in the cave, they would follow the scent of my blood. I struggled to my feet, bouncing from tree to tree to stay upright. My lungs ached with every step. Hot blood seeped down my back, sticking my shirt to me.

I leaned into the bark of the tree, coughing up crimson. The tang of copper penetrated my taste buds. I pushed off the tree to find another for support, then another. I kept moving until I thought my lungs would collapse.

I turned my head toward the distant sounds of humans. I tried to focus my vision, but it blurred. The smell of the female was strong. I could only assume she was a Hunter. No civilian would be this deep in the woods and not well armed to hunt us. Blood coated my back, urging me forward. I had to find her before I blacked out from the pain. The other wolves feared her. They knew crossing her path meant death, but I hoped it meant safety.

The rain splattered onto my head and soaked the grassy floor. I slipped on the ground, slamming into a newly created mud puddle. I had to stay awake just a little while longer.

I pulled myself to my feet, following her trail. She was close. I snapped my head to my left. She was in a tree. From the sound of her, she was attempting to climb down. I took a few more steps in her direction.

A horrid cough seized my lungs and shook my whole body. I struggled to pull in enough air as I continued to spit blood.

Her small frame was a blur as it slammed into the ground.

I instantly smelled her fear, but I couldn't be sure if she was afraid of me or the wolves closing in.

I stumbled a few more steps before collapsing face first into the soft earth. The last thing I saw was the red of her cloak swishing behind a tree before the world went dark.

Scarlet

The man—a Hunter, maybe—fell to the ground less than an arm's length away from where I stood, yet he didn't notice me standing there.

"Shh…," I whispered, kneeling. He jerked awake and looked up at me. His weary eyes peered through the shaggy dirty blonde hair that had fallen around his wide face. Blood and dirt caked his long locks, and crimson droplets were clinging to his short beard. Those deep-set, dark-brown eyes begged me for help. They seemed to lose focus again, as if he were struggling to stay conscious.

"I…I'm Scarlet. I can help you, if you let me," I spoke softly, inching my way toward him. He was lying chest down in the dirt with the tattered remains of his shirt around his massive biceps. The hole that tore through his back told me someone had hit him with an arrow.

"What were you doing out here?" I whispered to myself. I dragged my pack over to me, pulling out some cloth and cleaning fluid.

"This will hurt." The rain continued to pour around us, chilling my fingers and making it hard to move them. My frozen fingers struggled to tear the hole in his shirt wider and lightly touched his back before pouring the liquid to his wound. He clamped down his jaw hard and bucked against my touch as I tried to apply the bandage.

"You need to sit still," I snapped at him, a little rougher than I intended. He met my scolding with a deep rumble that vibrated through his body. "Have it your way," I spat back at him. I put my right knee to his spine.

I leaned all my weight onto him, pressing the soft cotton over the hole in his back.

"Now I gotta roll you over." He was growling at me. Actually growling—like a feral dog. "You gonna bite me if I let you up?"

I waited for the shake of his head before lifting my weight off his body.

"You are a lot bigger than me." I placed my hands under his chest and applied pressure trying to roll him over. "You're gonna need to help me." His skin scorched my fingertips. "How long ago were you shot? I think it's infected. You have a fever."

He grunted something that vaguely sounded like "now," but that couldn't be right. Pushing aside the thought, I braced for him to fight me when I flipped him.

"Ready?" Without waiting to hear his response, I pushed all my weight against him and began turning him onto his back. He rolled over with a thud, and I jumped to my feet, waiting for him to punch. His growl rumbled through me, bringing me to my knees again. "Damn. It doesn't look that bad. It didn't penetrate all the way through."

"Worse. Than. Looks," he said through gritted teeth. His breath came in short, heavy gasps.

"It's going to be okay," I breathed, stroking his hair. *What the hell?* I pulled my hand back quickly. *Just patch him up, and go to the inn…alone.*

Ignoring his panting, I leaned over him to inspect for any other injury. I flinched as he growled at me again.

I stood quickly. Every instinct in me told me to run like hell. This man was unlike any I'd ever seen. He was bigger and stronger than the Huntsmen, yet a small wound brought him to his knees. The Hunter in me wondered if he were a wolf, but that was impossible.

Once a man was infected, they became wolves for the rest of their days.

Even injured, this man could have killed me easily, but the worst he had done was growl. He was just an injured man who needed help.

Still, every instinct I had honed from all my winters spent in the forest told me to run.

He is just an injured villager. If I kept telling myself that, maybe I would actually begin to believe it.

"Will you be alright from here?" My voice shook as I spoke.

"I…I don't know." His eyes shut tight as he tried to sit up.

"Here. Let me help." I gripped his arm at the elbow and scooped my other hand behind his back. "Slowly."

He finally sat up, looking as green as summer grass. I helped him brace against a tree and stood beside him, throwing my pack over my shoulder.

I stood there for a moment, pondering the thought of helping him to the inn, but I had to hunt. It was my life. I needed to hunt like I needed to eat.

Run! my brain screamed. But the desire to flee was quickly drowned out by a softer voice.

Stay, she whispered.

The image of Rosemary's mangled body flashed in my mind. I fought back the tears that threatened to fall. The memory of her horrible death never got easier. *If I would have just helped her that day, maybe she'd still be alive.*

Over the winters, Rosemary had become my motivation. She was the reason I was a Huntsman. If not for her, I may have become someone else entirely— someone my parents had always wanted me to be.

The man's words came out in a whisper. "Don't. Please, don't leave me." For the first time, I could hear the terror in his voice.

He could hardly hold his head up. Rose's voice echoed in my head. *Don't let him suffer for your fear like you allowed me to suffer.*

"Fine," I spoke to the memory of my old friend.

"I think I can stand now." He didn't sound certain, but slowly he pulled himself to his feet, only to teeter to the side and fall against me. It took all my strength to stay upright.

I gripped the groaning man tight around his waist and grunted to myself. My old friend would never forgive me if I left this man here to die alone.

"Clearly, I can't leave you." I let his arms drape over my shoulders while I grasped him around his waist. The top of my head didn't even reach his chest, so he leaned forward as we walked.

Damn. He is thick. I grunted at his weight. *Nice and toned, but still.* I dismissed the flutter in my stomach at the thought that ran through my head.

"Can you walk? There's an inn not too far off."

"Th-thank you," he said hoarsely. With every haggard step, I knew I might have just fucked up my entire hunt for this season.

Conri

*H*er soft voice pulled me out of the darkness.

Scarlet.

Her brilliant green eyes were flecked with gold. Black, long strands clung to her face. They must be wet from the rain. She spoke, but I could not understand the words coming out of her mouth.

I lay with my chest in the mud, unable to free myself. A tearing noise came from just below my right ear.

My shirt?

The icy rain on my back told me she must have torn it.

Without warning, she poured a cold liquid on the wound that ripped through me like the arrow had. I kicked at her and tried to roll over.

But then a pressure weighed on my spine. She finished cleaning my back and placed something—a bandage, maybe—against my skin.

She cleaned the wound with a deftness I hadn't expected from a human. My gaze fell on the tree she'd been in. A crossbow sat gently against the trunk. Not just any human, but a Huntsman.

More words I couldn't quite hear came from her. Maybe something about a fever? About getting shot? I tried to tell her they might be all around us, but a blinding pain shot through me again as she flipped me over.

Was she laughing at me? That little bitch is actually fucking laughing at me. Wolfe growled.

My nails dug into my palms as I clenched my fists. I willed Wolfe to step back from my consciousness. *She's a Huntsman*, Wolfe growled at me. *That bitch would have us dead in a heartbeat if she knew what we were.*

She's the only reason we're not carrion, I snarled back at him. I squeezed harder, drawing blood. *And if you want to keep it that way, then back off.* Wolfe's hackles raised, and a deep, weary growl echoed inside me.

I locked eyes with our savior and my world shifted. The depth in her eyes stole my breath away.

She's... She can't be... Wolfe whispered in my mind.

No. I fought my urges and dragged my gaze from her face. *Shut the hell up Wolfe.*

Reluctantly, he backed into the darkness of my consciousness.

Her tiny hands inspected me for any other injury. Every nerve in my body screamed. Involuntarily, I growled at my savior.

As the pain eased, I tried to sit up, and a wave of nausea threatened to throw me back down. Her soft hands were pulling at me as she helped me to sit.

I stood, and the world spun around me. I thought I would find the ground again, but, to my surprise, the tiny woman caught me and supported my weight.

Scarlet

Thank the gods that the villagers were charitable by nature. I damn near collapsed once we reached town under the weight of my silent friend. Two of the farmers rushed over to help me as I staggered back through the town. They weren't as big as this man, but twice as big as I was. They stood there a moment, holding him, staring at me with their brows cocked while I caught my breath.

"Thank you," I finally managed to say.

"What happened?" one of the men asked.

"Not sure, but I plan to find out. Can you help him to the inn?"

They nodded, so I lead the way.

The inn had no name. It was just a wooden two-story building that stood in the center of town. It leaned a little to the side, as if a strong puff of air might blow it down.

I stepped into the front room while the villagers dragged him behind me. They deposited him into a chair. The stranger grumbled under his breath. The two men left in a rush. I watched the man slump back into the cushion that was so dirty I didn't think anyone would notice if he bled on it.

"I need two rooms, please," I told the tiny innkeeper. She instantly recognized me from before and backed away.

"I'm sorry, ma'am. I only have one room," she informed me. *I can't stay in the same room with a strange man.* I shot her my foulest look. "I-I'm sorry. It's our biggest room, though."

"Fine." I threw a few coins down and trudged back to my new roommate. He grew paler as I watched him. "What's your story?" I whispered to myself.

What the hell had I gotten myself into this time?

"H-here, ma'am. Your keys." The small girl practically threw them at me.

"Is there someone to help me get him to the room?"

"I can fetch the stable boy. He's strong enough." She spoke quickly and ran off toward the back.

Conri

I don't know how she managed to do it, but she dragged me all the way out of the forest. She passed me off to two men once we reached town, and they continued to help me walk. The chill of the rain was replaced with the warmth of the indoors. There were loud voices all around us, but they stopped suddenly as the strange hands released their hold on me.

Something hard pressed against my backside, and I wondered if I'd been propped in some sort of chair. Lights from the candles floated around me like stars. She might be small, but, damn, was she strong.

I couldn't hold my head up any longer and slumped over in the seat. Rubbing at my eyes, I struggled not to dry heave.

I heard her rough voice in the distance. She was clearly arguing with someone. May the gods help whoever opposed her. I must have laughed out loud, because she turned to glare at me.

"Fine," I heard her snap.

A minute later, I saw two of her and two of the new boy who seemed to appear out of nowhere.

"Come on. Let's get you upstairs."

I stifled the urge to vomit on her as she slid her shoulder under my arm. She wrapped an arm around my waist, enveloping me in her aroma.

They struggled under my weight up the narrow steps, having to angle themselves so we were shuffling up sideways. One person pushed while the other pulled. The pain in my back was nearly unbearable. I struggled to make my feet move, but I knew I wasn't being much help. A few times, I was sure we would tumble back down the stairs.

A huge boom forced me back from the darkness, and I realized it was the door slamming open. After a few seconds, I fell into something soft. I released a sigh of relief as I sank into the bed.

Scarlet

Between the boy and me, we couldn't have weighed fifteen stones. But we got the giant of a man into the bed.

The girl at the desk called this their biggest room—I'd hate to see their smallest. The man filled the bed, leaving his arms and feet hanging off the edge. A small chair sat in the corner opposite the door. It was pretty much exactly what you might expect from a village hidden deep in the forest and surrounded by death on all sides.

"Great. I gotta think of what to do with the strange man, and now I have no place to sleep," I mumbled to myself.

"No! Stop it! Let me go!" My *little* friend tossed and turned in the bed.

I jumped back, unsure of what to do. My mother always said, "Don't poke a sleeping dragon." And he was definitely a dragon of a man.

"I can't stay! Let me go!" He would wake the dead if he kept shouting.

"Easy now! You're safe." I inched my way toward him, which, in this room, took all of three steps. One of my hands grasped the hilt of my boot knife as I entered kicking distance. "You need to wake up." Gingerly, I touched his ankle. I jumped back, his foot narrowly missing me as he lashed out. He sat up quickly, looking around.

"Who are you?" he demanded. "Where am I?"

"You don't remember anything?" I backed away.

"I-I remember the woods. And you. That's it."

"I'm Scarlet...Kassidy. My name's Kassidy. After I patched you up, I brought you here, to this inn."

His face turned green as he tried to stand again.

"Thanks." He gasped, falling back to the bed, and he was out again.

"Shit." What had I gotten myself into? I moved to walk away when his fiery hands wrapped around my wrist. I looked back at him, but his eyes were still closed.

"Abrielle," he whispered as he pulled me so close that my face grazed his. He pressed his lips gently to mine like they were old friends. I froze. His soft lips moved against mine, pulling memories of Nate to the forefront of my mind. Fear quickly changed to rage at the intrusion but as quickly as it started, it was over. He dropped my hand and fell back to the bed.

I stormed out of the room, trying to ignore the heat rushing through my body. It wasn't the heat of rage but more like a foreign, desperate need. Too much time had passed since the heat of another body lay pressed against mine and, despite myself, I wanted this man even though he called me Abrielle. I had to get away from him. I would calm my breathing in the cool night air.

I pushed through the back door of the inn, pacing in front of the stables.

"What is his problem?" I asked the silence around me. "Yeah, he's hurt and probably won't even remember that, but still!" I jammed my hands into my crimson cloak trying to warm them up. The rain had stopped, leaving a permanent chill in the air.

I trudged down the muddy path out of town and toward the tree line. I longed to be back in the forest. People made me anxious. I rubbed at my middle as I paced.

A twig snapped in the distance. The hairs on the back of my neck stood, sending a chill down my spine. I froze where I stood, searching the woods for any sign I was being watched.

The wolves hated the Huntsmen as much as we hated them. I couldn't see anyone watching, but that didn't mean they weren't out there. I reached around for my crossbow before remembering I left it back in the room.

"Fuck," I whispered to myself. Backing away from the trees, I tried to control my breathing. I didn't dare turn my back until I reached the edge of town.

I slowed my pace, avoiding the strange looks from the villagers on the road.

My heart still raced by the time I got back to the room. My eyes fell once again to the giant stranger asleep on the bed. I kept a wary eye on him as I strode across the room to peer out the window.

"What are the wolves doing so close to town?" I asked softly. "It's too early in the season for them to attack a place like this." I paced again in the tiny room. "I didn't see anyone, but...I know they were there. Why?"

The beast of a man twitched in the bed. My eyes lingered over him. Question after question raced through my mind. I gazed back out the window toward the dark forest in the distance.

Whoever shot him had nearly killed him. It couldn't be a coincidence that something stalked the woods now. I looked back at him. Were they hunting him? He tossed on the bed again, slamming his fist into the wall behind him. He howled at the pain in his arm.

"Hush now." I tiptoed over to him, hoping he wouldn't wake. His wrist was warm in my hands as I lifted it and placed it by his side. "You gotta be easy. You're healing."

49

I am speaking to an unconscious man.

Shaking my head, I rolled him over slightly to peel back the tape from one corner of the bandage. "You're fine for now, but keep thrashing, and this will definitely start bleeding again." I smoothed the bandage back down over his back. My eyes lingered over his torn shirt that hugged tight to his chest and exposed patches of flesh.

I had never seen muscles so defined, not even among the Huntsmen.

He let out a moan as I dragged my hand slowly off his flesh.

"Kassidy." He whispered my given name like a lover.

My stomach fluttered at the tenderness in his voice causing me to I stumble back and sank into the chair in the corner of the room.

6
Fighting Ghosts
Conri

I snapped my eyes open at the sudden pressure on my arm. Heat radiated from the wound at my shoulder and I clamped my jaw shut to keep from screaming. A lavender scent washed a sense of calm over me, even as my body ached.

My muscles were weak and burning leaving me at her mercy. Blinking the pain away I focused on my surroundings. I lay on my back on a lumpy bed in a shabby room. A hand shook my side. *She saved me.* She jumped slightly as I growled.

"You need to help me." She nudged my side. "Have you always been such a baby?"

"Piss off." The words escaped my gritted teeth before I could stop them.

"Oh, and a wise ass too, eh?" She laughed. "Look, I get that it hurts, but I gotta do this. You have to help me. You gotta roll over so I can check your bandage." She nudged my side with her knee again. "Don't make me do it alone again."

Her cool hands slid under my back, coaxing me on to my side. With great effort, I continued rolling over until I was flat on my chest.

I grunted as she tore the bandage from my back in one swift motion. Her gentle touch came as she cleaned my wound. A few seconds later, there was a gentle pressure as she placed something soft over the wound.

The edge of my vision blurred as the darkness consumed me again.

Scarlet

The mud caked to my body made my skin itch. My companion was fast asleep, so I headed for the shower house with fresh clothes.

A small, open-walled building stood behind the inn with a large tank sitting on the roof with a copper tube wrapped around it. The tubing connected to a wood-fed boiler heating the water as it flowed down to the shower head. I loathed everything about public bathhouses, but it was better than the icy river. The warm water washed away my aches.

I will spend all my savings if I don't get back out there soon.

I sighed. Normally I spent all hunting season outside. Occasionally, I'd come into town for a shower and a hot meal, but I'd already paid for three nights, and only the gods knew how much more time I'd be here. I had a small amount saved to help get me through the season, and I was wasting it on a nameless man.

I turned the water off and reached for a clean set of clothes from my bag. "I'll give him until the full moon, then I'm gone," I promised myself.

I opened the door to my little room. Silence echoed around the tiny space causing me to drop my pack on the floor. He was gone.

Maybe he left? Both hope and disappointment filled me, leaving a wrenching in my gut.

The sound of something I could only describe as a growl shook the windows of my room, startling me. I ran toward the window. In the shadows below, I just barely made out his figure towering over the work horses that bolted past him. He stood in the middle of the road, swinging his arms wildly. He'd torn his tattered shirt off and was brandishing it like a sword at the townsfolk as they ran from him.

"Fuck me." I bolted from the room, taking the stairs two at a time.

When I reached the road, my heart fell at the fear in his eyes. My strange patient had dropped the shirt and swung his fists in the air. I watched for a second, confusion overwhelming me. A growl that shook my chest emanated from him as he fought off unseen foes.

I looked around for someone, anyone, who would be strong enough to tame the man, but the street was now empty. Faces peered out from behind the glass of nearby windows, but no one dared step outside.

"You…can't take us…back. We won't…let you!" His ragged breathing made him hard to understand. He whipped his head back and forth, snapping and snarling. His eyes were open, but there was a crazed, fearful look in them as if he wasn't really here.

He's fighting whoever shot him.

"Hey! Knock it off! You're scaring people," I yelled, hoping to snap him from the hallucinations holding him.

He stared right through me. Suddenly, his massive fist careened toward my face. I ducked just in time, the whoosh of air passing mere inches above my head.

"You need to wake up before you hurt someone!" I shouted at him, avoiding his fists. "Namely me," I spoke to myself. I stepped closer. He shoved me to the ground. My back hit the road hard, knocking the air from my lungs. Catching my breath, I stood.

"You wanna play it that way? Okay then." I stepped back and raised my fists.

"We won't face the trials. Not for him, and most certainly not for you." He threw another punch. I blocked this blow with my forearm, wincing at the strength of his hit.

"I don't know what the trials are, but I won't take you anywhere except back to the inn." I tried to calm him, but his eyes looked far away.

I danced around him, dipping and diving, to avoid every new jab. Slowly, I moved closer.

"You need to wake up!" I shouted again, hoping to snap him out of it.

He shook his head as I spoke, like he was trying to rid himself of the images plaguing him.

"Please," I begged.

His eyes grew cold and his body rigid.

"No!" he screamed before he charged me again.

I ducked under his arm and spun quickly behind him, using my foot to push against his lower back. The man crashed to the ground with a thud.

He moaned where he'd fallen. I leaned over him and pressed my hand to his cheek, the scratch of his beard against my palm. Immediately I yanked my hand back at his fever.

"Oh, man. You gotta help me. Please, just come back to the inn with me."

His eyes looked up at me. He rolled over in the dirt with a wild grin.

"Hey, pretty lady. You say something about an inn?" He stood, stumbling a bit before regaining his bearings. His gaze seemed to linger, as if he were taking me all in. A different kind of growl purred up from his throat, one sent shivers down my spine as my body tingled at the lustful sound.

Still, I rolled my eyes. He was delusional. I wrapped an arm around him as I led him back to the inn. He staggered as he walked, but I held on tight.

Slowly, taking long pauses for each step, we made our way back up to my room. He collapsed on the edge of the bed with little effort on my part.

His lustful stare found me again, and before I could pull away, his hands wrapped around my waist, pulling me to his chest. His mouth scorched against my skin as he rained kisses along my neck. I practically giggled at the roughness of his beard tickling me. My breath caught in my throat as he pressed his lips just above my breasts. My body begged him to not stop but I knew he wasn't aware of his actions. I had to suppress a grin as I shoved him off.

Plenty of drunken idiots had hit on me over the winters. Though I was no great beauty, I was certainly pretty enough for a single night. Most men ran the second they saw my crossbow. Sometimes they were too drunk or too determined to take no for an answer. When that happened, they would run even faster when I pressed one of my knives against their most prized possession.

"Aw, come on, gorgeous. Let's get naked and run through the woods." He trailed a finger down the inside of my wrist, before wrapping his long fingers around the sensitive skin. I suppressed the shiver that ran down my spine as he pulled me toward him again.

"You're deranged, and you need sleep," I said, before I shoved him back to the bed. He didn't fight me. In fact, I think he was asleep before he hit the pillow.

Mercifully, he slept in silence for the next few hours. I perched myself along the bed shortly after he fell asleep. The heat of the fever reached for me, and soon I found myself sweating too.

Each time I rested a cool cloth against his brow, within a few moments I needed to refresh the towel. Worry settled in my stomach.

How could someone survive a fever such as this?

I rolled him onto his side to change his bandage, and that's when I noticed that the sheets were sopping wet from the sweat pouring out of him.

"It's only been a few moonrises since I found you. Why is there no sign of healing?"

The thought of running and leaving him here crossed my mind about a thousand times. I was wasting my time and money here caring for this stranger, but I knew he would die if I left him with these backwoods folks.

Once again, I watched his ragged breathing.

I should run.

The thought crossed my mind again, but something about this man was different. I had spent my life running from any kind of connection to another human. My own parents kept me at arm's length; they never understood me. But this man…I couldn't stop looking at him. He looked so vulnerable in this bed that was much too tiny for him.

His pitiful moans tore at my heart. Each of his whimpers or flinches from pain brought me back to the edge of the bed. He kept me there, watching over him, protecting him, and I didn't even know his name. I wanted to run from what was stirring deep within me, yet I couldn't force my feet forward.

"Shhh," I tried to calm him.

A foul scent hit my nose, bringing up my recent meal. I swallowed hard and leaned in closer. I pulled one corner of the bandage up. The odor grew stronger as some yellow, oozing liquid stuck to the cloth.

I fetched the medical kit from my pack. I pulled out some witch hazel and a bottle filled with a fine, silvery powder. The mattress sank beneath me as I sat back on the bed. He snapped awake, his eyes wide with panic.

"What is that?" he asked through gritted teeth.

"It-it's silver oxide. The wound is infected. I need to scrub it clean and put some of this in it to clear it up." I had never had to clean a wound this bad before. I wasn't sure my stomach could handle it.

"No… silver…" He twisted around, trying to look at me. "Something…still in it." His shoulders trembled.

I set the bottle down and watched his face. What was he afraid of? I needed to clean out the infection, even if he wouldn't let me.

"Please… get it out," he breathed.

I leaned over him, examining the wound. With two fingers, I poked around the hole and jumped back.

He was right. There was a hard lump just under his muscles.

"Fuck." My stomach turned over. "You need a healer." I told him.

"No…can't trust them." He shut his eyes tight.

"And you can trust *me*?" I questioned.

"Please, Kassy." His eyes snapped open, and I could see the pain he was fighting back. It sent chills down my spine. "I need your help."

"Shit," I whispered. I was going to have to dig it out myself.

I slunk downstairs and asked the innkeeper for the largest bottle of whiskey she could find.

I took a swig of the bottle before stepping back into the room. I wished I had something better than my two hands and a knife to pull the arrow from his back.

He lay in the bed fighting invisible enemies again. I paced the little room holding the bottle tight before steeling my nerves and opening the whiskey again. I closed my eyes and took another long swig. Swallowing hard and shaking off the burn in my throat, I walked to the bed.

"Hey," I whispered to him. "Can you take a drink of this? It'll help." I sat on the edge of the bed and lowered the bottle to his lips. "Please?"

He drank half the bottle in one breath.

"Okay, that's enough." I pulled the bottle away and grabbed my knife.

The man flinched.

"Listen, the broadhead is still in you and I gotta cut it out, but you gotta promise me you won't attack me."

Even through his pain, I watched the small smile grow at the corner of his mouth.

"Fair enough," he sighed.

He rolled onto his stomach, gripping the edges of the bed. I crawled onto the bed and straddled his hips, holding him down as best I could.

"Ready?"

I wasn't sure if I was asking more for him or for myself. I peeled the fresh bandage from his back and poured a little of the amber liquid over the blade, letting it spill onto his wound. He jerked in response.

"Damn." He was too strong, even with the alcohol. I pinned one knee against his spine and leaned over him. "This is going to hurt. Please don't kill me."

The blade shook in my hand as I laid it on his skin. I searched for the arrowhead with my hand and traced my path with the knife. Fresh blood and pus oozed from the new cut. He screamed through gritted teeth as I dug deeper. Metal scraped against metal, so I retracted my blade.

"Okay... now for the fun part." I breathed, setting down my knife. Animal blood was one thing, but this was human. There was nothing different about blood. It was all hot and viscous, but knowing it came from a human made my skin crawl.

My stomach turned again at the smell that lingered on his infected wound. Closing my eyes, I plunged my fingers into his exposed muscles. I fought the urge to vomit as blood and pus coated my hand.

He bucked his hips, but I leaned all my weight down harder on his back so he wouldn't send me hurtling toward the floor. Mercifully, it took mere moments for me to find the broad head. I pinched at the smooth shaft of what remained of the arrow with my finger and thumb.

"I don't know how to do this other than to pull. I'm sorry."

"Just do it," he grunted.

In one swift movement, I yanked it out. A deep rumble came from within him as he screamed into the bed. His screams faded, and I knew he was unconscious.

"Thank the gods," I whispered. I walked back to my med kit, dropping the broadhead to the floor. Cleaning out his wounds would be much easier now that he was out.

Conri

I woke to a light pressure on my back and inhaled her intoxicating aroma before slowly opening my eyes. My body instantly relaxed at her scent. Her face came into focus. Her golden skin looked duller than I had remembered from before, and dark circles now encased her eyes.

"Good morning." Kassidy yawned as she stretched her lean arms above her head. Something stirred inside of me as I watched her body move to stand.

"Morning." I stretched out my hand toward her, inviting her to sit. "How long?"

"It's only been six moonrises since I first found you." She dropped the arrowhead on the bed beside me. I eyed it, making sure it didn't touch my skin. If she knew what I was, I'm sure I'd be dead already. I breathed out as I looked back up at her as she continued. "I should have left you for dead. It would have saved me a lot of headache. Who are you? And why did I have to pull this nasty broadhead outta your back? Who the hell wanted to kill you so badly?" She gave me a hard stare that forced my guilt to the surface.

I sat up, careful not to touch the silver, and watched her. Her eyes bore into me. She wouldn't be convinced as easily as others would be. She was a Huntsman, would she believe the lie? *Would my magic really work on her?* I reached for it before I spoke. The familiar tingle in my fingertips lingered before I forced myself to project my magic toward her.

"It was a mistake," I said. "A green Hunter saw me walking in the woods and shot me." The lie burned my throat. She stared at me for a long moment with hardened eyes before they softened and her body let out the tension she was holding.

I hadn't used my Sage magic on a human in a long time, and it disgusted me to use it on her. My stomach soured and I vowed to never do that again. She sat on the end of the bed and looked me over.

"I've spent all this time watching out for a man, and I don't even know his name. My mother would be angry with me. I've had to do some pretty disgusting things, ya know." Her voice turned playful as she spoke.

"I know. I remember. I'm sorry for the trouble I've caused you. My name's Conri." I turned over, laying gently on my back. "I cannot begin to thank you. You saved my life." Something pulled me towards her and I swore in that moment I'd never use my magic on this human again, even if she chose to kill me.

Her face softened as she turned her eyes away from me. "I… You're welcome."

Her heart rate increased as I clasped her hand in mine and said, "I mean it. I am indebted to you. And I don't forget my debts." This one human was unlike any other I'd met in my long history. Even Wolfe settled at her touch. Everything in my blood called me to be near her. Almost without thinking about it, I brought her hand to my lips. "What can I do to repay you?"

She jerked her hand out of my grasp, standing to her feet. She tried to hide it, but I saw the flush in her cheeks before she turned away.

"It's nothing. Really."

I sat up in the bed slowly, looking around the room. It was small and dingy, with hardly enough space for the two of us. "My life is not nothing. I owe you more than you know." I winced at the pain as I tried to stand, and I fell back into the bed.

She jumped to my side. "Damn it. You're still healing. If you ruin the hard work I put into saving your life, I'll kill you myself." Her eyes met mine and my breath caught in my throat as if she could see right through to my soul. My arms ached to hold her and my lips burned to touch hers.

I need to claim her. Wolfe spoke.

My hand reached out on its own, as if Wolfe were in control. I cupped her face in my hands and pulled her closer.

She didn't fight against my touch. She leaned into it. I couldn't stop myself as I pressed my lips gently to hers. Her lips moved with mine, begging for more, but I had to control Wolfe before he took it too far. I pushed his desires down and pulled away before I gave in.

"Thank you, Kassy." I breathed in her sweet smell, resting my forehead on hers. That brief contact wasn't enough. I longed to taste her lips again and again. Every bit of her called me to her. It wasn't just her body I longed to be near. She was beautiful, yes, but her soul called to me. I needed to know her deeper than just a physical connection. I had never experienced such a strong pull toward another person, let alone a human. Wolfe would have taken her at that moment, but I pulled away.

"You smell of lavender," I inhaled deeply.

She sniffed her hair. "Oh yeah. That'd be my mother's soaps. I don't normally use them out in the forest..." A yawn erupted from her gorgeous lips.

Releasing her, I stood to my feet. "You need to rest. Take the bed. I'll send the innkeep up with fresh sheets, then go find us some food." Her eyes filled with sadness, and my heart shattered as she looked away. She fidgeted with her hair before she turned her back to me and sat in the chair in the corner.

I took a deep breath for the first time in days. My body was healing, all thanks to Kassidy. I looked back at the small woman and watched her for a moment. She pulled her knees to her chest and rested her head on them. I suppressed the desire to pick her up and throw her body into the bed, lie against the curve of her back, and bury my face in her dark locks. I dragged my eyes away from her and forced my feet out the door.

My chest ached to be away from her. I couldn't shake the desire to be with her. But she was just a human. Nothing special about her... right? I wanted to believe it was simply a need to be filled, but I knew there was more. I needed air.

I walked out of the inn as fast as I could without causing a scene. The crisp morning air chilled my bare chest. I headed off the main path and straight for the graveyard at the edge of the forest. Even in this small town, I knew there'd be one crypt.

I strode up to the solitary concrete structure. Before I entered, I scanned the area to make sure no one followed or watched. Not many would venture this close to the woods, even to visit the dead, but still, I had to make sure.

Only when I was completely alone did I shift my hand into a paw and pressed it into the door. A lock clicked open. I pushed the door and found the hidden stairs to the supply room. We made sure long ago that no wolf would be left in the cold when they needed to be human. The secret underground storage rooms were filled with everything a human could ever need, yet no human could ever find. When I reemerged, I had fresh clothes and coins to spare.

I stepped back into the light and walked quickly out of the graveyard. My keen hearing picked up the sounds of fighting. Metal clanged on metal and the grunts of two, maybe three, people emanated from the other end of town. Men rushed toward the sounds. I looked at the inn. The window where Kassy slept was still dark.

I followed the others. I couldn't suppress a laugh when I arrived. Kassy wielded a blade nearly as long as she was tall and was fighting off two men twice her size. They danced around a circular wall of stone with a sand floor.

She was barefoot and wearing loose-fitting pants and a top that fit tight to her chest, leaving her stomach exposed, her red cloak lay draped over the short wall. My breath caught in my throat watching her. Her feet twirled like a graceful dancer, but her arm swung the sword down like the deadliest assassin I'd ever seen. I leaned against the waist-high wall and watched her in both terror and in awe.

Her blade stopped inches from her opponent's face. He dropped his sword and fell to his knees. She spun her weapon to the other man, who was attempting to sneak up behind her. He, too, dropped his sword in defeat. They both bowed and whispered, "Scarlet," before they turned and walked away.

I stood and clapped my hands slowly. She dropped the sword as she looked at me. Her face turned even redder than it was before as her chest heaved for breath, and sweat poured from her.

"I'm impressed," I told her. I had seen some amazing fighters in my time, but none as captivating as her. Wolfe begged me to bed her and my cock stiffened as she walked closer.

"I couldn't sleep, so I went for a walk. This town doesn't have much of a guard, and what they do have is pretty green. The lieutenant saw me, and asked if I could spar with the younger ones." She shrugged and turned her gaze to the ground.

I raised her chin with a finger. "Never be ashamed or embarrassed by who you are." She tried to look away, but I held her face firm. "Do you understand me? You are beautiful and fierce, and you better never change a thing."

She leaned in and kissed me. I was so taken aback by the tenderness of her lips I hardly moved. She pulled away too quickly.

"Sorry," she whispered.

I reached for her sides before she could walk away and pulled her back to me. "Never apologize either." I captured her lips with mine, returning the tenderness. I was thankful for the short wall between us, or I might have taken her right then and there.

I reluctantly released her, letting my hands fall to my sides. We stared at each other for a long moment before she finally spoke.

"I think… I think I really am tired now. Will you walk with me?"

I scooped her up by the waist and over the wall and set her down softly on the other side. She allowed me to guide her gently with my hand on her back. Her skin on my skin woke every nerve in my body. She nudged me every once in a while as we walked, as if she couldn't walk in a straight line.

"Where'd you get the shirt?" she finally asked.

I looked down. "Oh this? I had some coin, so I bought a new one." More lies.

She shrugged and kept walking.

We walked in silence up to the door of the room we shared. I blocked the doorway, cupping her face in my hand. My thumb caressed her mouth. She closed her eyes, tilted her head, and parted her lips. Her hands rested on my hips. My cock stiffened as her fingers dipped under my shirt, grazing my skin. I breathed deep, fighting Wolfe's desire to follow her inside. Leaning down, I kissed her forehead and stepped back.

"Get some sleep. I think I need to walk some more." I turned and walked off before Wolfe could change my mind.

8
The Harvest Festival
Scarlet

he aroma of seasoned steak and freshly baked rolls woke me. Sitting up, I heard the faint sounds of a knife scraping a plate. A plate of food and silverware sat on the edge of the bed. I scanned the room for Conri until I found him sitting in the chair with food of his own. He ate silently. My stomach grumbled loudly.

I reached for the plate and pulled it back to me. I put as much distance between me and Conri as possible. There was an odd desire to be near him, but he was still a stranger. I leaned against the back wall before cutting into the sizzling meat.

"How long was I asleep?" I asked between bites.

"Well, this is my third meal of the day." He didn't look up from his own food as he sat on the chair eating. "How long have you been out in the woods hunting?"

"How do you know I'm a Hunter?"

"The crossbow and all the silver gave it away," he shrugged.

"Most people don't believe a woman can be a Huntsman."

"Most people haven't had you take care of them. I believe you're capable of anything." He smiled at me, and my stomach fluttered.

I gulped down my food before I spoke again. I wasn't used to men smiling at me like he was. Normally, their smiles meant they thought I'd fail. But his smile... I had to reorder the thoughts in my head before I could think clearly again. "I'm not even sure how long it's been since I left home," I said, wiping the juices from the meat off my chin. "Normally I sleep in the trees."

He finally looked up at me. "I've never known a Hunter that took their job that seriously. You must be good at it." He placed his knife and fork on his plate before placing it down on the floor. "Is hunting all you do?"

I swallowed hard. Something about this man made me crazy. He didn't look at me like other men in my life had. My fellow Huntsmen looked through me as if I weren't there. Even the few men I had been with only saw money when they looked at me. Only Nate had shown me love, but he was gone. I had never really shared my life with a stranger. There was no one in my life I trusted enough to confide in.

So why do I want to tell him everything about me?

"When I was nine, I watched my best friend get slaughtered by a wolf. My Saba started training me the very next day. It's all I've ever known.". The sudden memory turned my stomach and I set my food aside.

He was at my side with one long stride. His weight on the edge of the bed jostled me, forcing me to rearrange myself. I swung my legs over the side and edged a little closer. My heart quickened as he rested his hand beside my thigh.

"I'm sorry you had to see that. Some wolves can be vicious."

"Some?" I scoffed. "There's no such thing as a kind wolf."

"You might be right." His voice was thick with emotion as he released a long sigh. He looked down at his hands before wiping them on the sheet, as if rubbing off the memory of something that had been there before.

"You sound like you've known your fair share of violence."

"Yeah…" He stared at the wall across from us, and he looked as if his mind drifted to a faraway place.

"I…" I didn't know what to say, so I just placed my hand on top of his. He curled his fingers around mine. His shoulders rose as he ran his free hand through his hair. Slowly, he seemed to come back from whatever haunted him.

"Thanks." His eyes shimmered with unshed tears when he finally looked at me again.

"How are you feeling? Your shoulder, I mean."

"Better, thanks to you."

"I only did what I thought was right. Who shot you?"

"I have my suspicions about who it was. I can't go home, so I can't be certain." He pulled his hand away and shifted in the bed so he was looking at me.

"Why can't you go home?"

"I'm not welcome. Whoever shot me was from my home."

"I'm sorry." My stomach dropped remembering the long glances as I walked back into camp the next year after Nate. " I can't imagine that. I mean, the people back home are afraid of me, but at least I have a home." I turned to face him as well. "So... are you a Hunter then?"

"I... No, I am not."

"I'd ask what you do, but I don't think you'd tell me, anyway."

"Probably for the best." He rubbed his arm.

"So, if you can't go home, what will you do?"

"Not sure. Guess I need to figure that out." His gaze fell away as he continued. "I'm sorry."

"For?"

"I've been remembering some of the things I did in my delirium..." His face flushed slightly.

I said nothing, but warmth rushed to my cheeks. I thought back to his hunger in that first kiss.

He stood when I didn't respond and walked back to the chair to pick up his plate. "Finish eating. There's something I want to show you."

Once outside, he led the way through town. Laughter and music filled the cool evening air. I looked around for the source. This was a modest town, but I couldn't tell where the noise was coming from yet.

He chuckled beside me, grasping my right hand, and pulling me forward. We came to the edge of the tiny village before I saw the massive white tent. Food vendors and game booths surrounded the gigantic structure. I paused, pulling on his arm.

I hadn't seen a festival like this in many winters. With the wolf population diminishing, it was like a small bit of joy had finally returned to the village.

"I know you'll have to get back to the hunt soon, but I wanted to show my gratitude. If I only get this night, I want to make it special." He gently tugged on my arm.

"How... How did you even know this was here? You've been laid up in bed," I questioned him.

"When you were sleeping... I went for a walk to stretch my legs a bit, and came across it. I might have done a little scouting for some way to repay you for the kindness you've shown me." He stopped walking and watched me.

Every nerve in my body vibrated.

My village hadn't bothered with anything like this for several winters. The last time they had celebrated was when I was barely nine winters old. It was the last Harvest Festival before everything changed. Enjoying attractions with Rose and her brother, Nate. Eating foods our family would never have been able to make at home. That was the last memory I had where I was truly happy—just a few weeks before I would find her mangled body.

I wanted to simultaneously run toward and also far away from the music. I closed my eyes to push out that last memory and focus on the good ones. My inner child was winning the battle as curiosity flooded me. My breathing slowed, and I smiled at him.

"We can always leave, if you need to," he said. He threaded his fingers with mine as if he saw right through me to the trauma within.

"I haven't been to a festival since I was a little girl," My voice shook as I spoke. I wanted to go, but my feet refused to move. I stared off into the distance at the lights dancing. Laughter rose, lifting my heart. These people that had lost so much took the time to celebrate the little things. Why shouldn't I?

I stepped closer to Conri, letting go of my fear.

"Well, you are in for a treat, then. What shall we do first?" His voice was lighter than back in the inn.

"Um… what games do they have?"

He laughed at my excitement. "This way. I know the perfect game."

I followed his lead as we walked toward the festival. The townsfolk were dressed in their best clothes. Women wore colorful dresses that hugged every curve, and the men wore dark pants and long coats. Even the children were clean and wearing nice clothes.

The music seemed to emanate from the center, and I wondered if a band was playing. No one stopped to stare as we walked past them, and I felt almost normal. Not a Huntsman, not the legend Scarlet, but just a girl. I walked a little closer to Conri, letting him wrap his arm around me. His strong, earthy aroma surrounded me, helping me realize I was home in his arms.

People walked around, munching on meat on sticks and custard pastries, while others stopped to play various games, from Knock the Pins, to a fishing game. We stopped in front of a narrow but long shooting range. Two small bows sat on top of the table.

"Ah, you look like a shooter, son. Trying to win a prize for your lady?" the game master shouted above the crowd.

"She's not my lady… not yet, at least." Conri turned to grin at me. My stomach flipped again, and heat rose to my face. "And she's the actual shooter." He pulled me forward.

"Good. Good. Let's see the lady shoot. You care to join her? Make it a friendly competition?"

"Sure. Let's say… If I win, I get a kiss?" he asked me.

I grinned wickedly. "If I win, you ride the Ferris wheel with me."

His eyes widened, and he swallowed hard, but he placed a few coins on the table and picked up the bow. My stomach soured slightly at his hesitation. Looking down at myself, I noticed that my figure was not as dainty as other women, and I wondered if his aversion had been toward me. But why should I care what this man thought? He was right. I should be leaving in the morning anyway. I turned my attention back to the table.

I looked at him. "Where'd you get the coin from?"

"It was in my pack. I'm running a bit low, so I guess I will need to find a way to earn some more quickly."

I eyed him skeptically for a moment before turning back to the fair game.

Stepping up to the table, I picked up the bow. I then grabbed five arrows and laid four out on the table. I took aim and fired one right after the other. He was still struggling with the tiny bow. When he finally fired all five arrows, I focused my eyes on the target ahead of me. Five arrows protruded near the center for me, and his target was empty.

I couldn't help but laugh. "I figured you'd be a bit better of a shot than that." We set the bows down, and I looked at him. His smile faded. "Shit!" I only now thought of his injury.

"No, ma'am. I am a terrible shot. Not to mention my back is throbbing," Conri said while wincing.

"Oh shit! I'm so sorry. I forgot. Are you alright?" I closed the gap, reached around him, and gingerly touched his back. "What can I do?"

He wrapped his good arm behind my back, pulling me to his chest. "You could feel sorry enough for me that you say I won?" he grinned.

I shoved out of his grasp and laughed. "No way. You are getting on that Ferris wheel," I said as I strode past him to where the ride stood.

The ride was the tallest thing I'd ever seen. The steam engine powering the belts and pulley system vibrated through my body and drowned out the sounds of the people at the top of the wheel.

Conri finally caught up to me as I stood on the ground looking up watching the wooden wheel slow down. He looked up and froze.

Stepping next to him, I took his hand. "Are you scared?" I asked when he shook.

"I've never been fond of heights." He stepped forward anyway.

The carnie locked the wooden bar in front of us and started the ride again. Conri's body tensed next to mine. I took his arm and pulled it over my shoulder and edged closer to him. He seemed to relax slightly.

"You can hold on to me if you're scared." I prodded him. What was I thinking? Flirting with a man I hardly knew. I needed to get back to the hunt. But his warmth spread into me, and I forgot all about my mission. I just wanted to lean into him.

The ride stopped at the top, sending a fresh wave of panic through Conri's muscles. I ran my hand up his body trying to release some of his tension. His jaw tensed and his chest rose and fell in quick bursts. My heart beat faster and faster. I let my hand raise to his cheek and pulled his eyes to mine.

"How about I feel sorry enough for you to let you win?" I asked him.

He stared at me wide eyed for a long moment before I pulled his face to mine and kissed him gently. His mouth didn't move with mine at first, but then his hand gripped me by the base of my neck, and he pulled me into him. Heat flooded my body more intensely than it had in many winters. I parted my lips slightly, letting his tongue graze them. Every nerve buzzed to life. My heart stopped when our tongues met. I pulled away, startled by the desire that bloomed within me. It wasn't as if this were the first kiss I'd ever had but it was as if his kiss meant life. Without his touch, there was nothing, and that alone scared me more than any wolf hunt ever had.

"A pity kiss?" He rasped out.

The hurt in his voice shattered my walls and I needed him more than I'd ever needed anyone. I swallowed hard and grasped him by the nape of his neck, pulling him into a deeper kiss. I didn't care that we were high in the sky, I pulled at his shirt, untucking it from his pants, and ran my hands up his chest. His arms wrapped around me, pulling me tighter. I parted my lips slightly, inviting him in then draped my leg over his lap when the car rocked.

His arms clasped me so tightly I strained to breathe. I pushed away, slapping at his chest.

"Can't... breathe..." I gasped.

"S–sorry." He eased off his grasp. "For a moment there, I forgot we were ludicrously endangering our lives for fun."

I let his arm fall back onto my shoulder, and I snuggled against his chest. I didn't care that my mother would say I was acting ridiculous, but his arms were home, more so than my own home had ever been. I'd grown tired of paying for companionship. It was unnatural. But this... this was comfortable.

Once the ride stopped and we found solid ground again, I asked him, "What would you like to play next? I'd hate to beat you at another game."

"Um... How about Knock the Pins?"

"Fair enough. I can't throw a ball to save my life."

A few people were in line for the game, so I leaned into him until he pulled me in front of him, wrapping his arms around me. Warmth spread throughout my body, and I couldn't stop a smile from spreading. People passed us and smiled. They actually smiled at me. Since dawning the red cape, I hadn't smiled at a single stranger, but here in this small town with this man, I could see myself having a normal life and maybe make a friend or two. I nuzzled into him, dreaming of a life outside of the Huntsman ways.

"So, what kind of bet we gonna make this time?" he asked.

I jabbed him in the ribs with my elbow. "I think we should steer clear of betting against one another."

His chest rumbled with laughter. "Fair enough."

He stepped up to the table and gave the man a coin before tossing one ball at the stack of pins. My jaw dropped. With a loud crash, all nine pins went flying off the shelf, and landed on the ground. He didn't leave a single one standing. The game master looked a little miffed as he handed Conri the wooden horse figurine he'd asked for.

We walked through the games toward a large tent in the center. Just before the entrance sat an old woman with an easel and some paint. My mind drifted back to before Rose's death as I watched her paint the little boy sitting on the seat in front of her. Her shaky hands steadied the moment the brush met his cheek and the boy sat perfectly still as she drew.

"You want a picture painted?" Conri's deep voice pulled me out of my trance.

"W-What?" It took me a moment to hear what he asked. "No. I... I just... never mind." I pulled away from his grasp and walked away.

"Kassy! Wait up! What's wrong?" He gripped my shoulder, pulling me to a stop. I quickly wiped the tears from my eyes before I turned to face him. "What?" he asked again.

"It's just... gah.... What is it about you that makes me want to confess my entire life to you?" I spat a little harsher than intended before walking off again. I didn't want the villagers to see me cry. I got clear of the festival and made my way toward the trees.

Conri didn't speak, but I knew he was behind me.

"I haven't drawn since I joined the Huntsmen. I used to love it, but death changes a person. Even if it's the death of an enemy. I burned everything the night I got home after my first hunt. I have seen nothing worth drawing...." I turned to face those dark eyes and his shaggy hair. He stood an arm's length away respecting my space, but his eyes begged to be closer. "Until I saw you stumbling through the woods."

I stood there, staring at him. Something kept nagging at the back of my brain to run. Something wasn't right with him. He was too strong. He healed too quickly. And clearly someone wanted him dead.

So why is the rest of me aching to wrap my arms around him? Why do I want to press my body against his and forget the world existed outside of us?

My heart won the argument, and I stepped into his arms. His scent reminded me of being in the trees. I had found my home in the forest. I had found my purpose amongst the trees, and his arms wrapped around me was like coming home again.

I pushed back just enough to see his face. Tears filled his eyes.

My mind raced as I pulled at the collar of his shirt until his rough lips found mine. I reached my hands up, running my fingers through his silky hair. His massive hands grasped my ass, lifting me off the ground. He didn't even flinch at my weight in his arms. Wrapping my legs around his waist, I deepened my kiss. He sighed into my mouth and let our tongues meet.

Wetness built between my thighs at his touch. He rumbled with a growl from deep within and pulled away from the kiss. He buried his face in my neck, tickling me with his coarse beard, grazing the tip of his tongue around the edge of my ear, sending shivers down my spine. I gasped, clinching my legs tighter around him.

He moved us deeper into the woods until the trees obscured the sunlight. My back found solid bark before he resumed his teasing.

Licking the corners of my mouth, he said, "You're killing me, Kassy."

I pressed my lips to his gently. "How's that?"

He growled, "I told myself I'd never fall for a woman again. And here you are, driving all my senses mad." He devoured me before I could respond. His heart raced so aggressively, its movement tapped against my chest. Heat exploded in my core as he kissed my neck. His fingers found the edge of my shirt slipping under it. His hot hands caressed my stomach, sending fire through me.

I reached between us, over the soft leather of his pants, and stroked his hardened cock. He quickly gripped my wrist, pulling it away.

"What's wrong? I know you want it," I said, my breath ragged.

"I-I just can't." He let me down gently and turned away.

"Wait! I'm sorry!"

He walked deeper into the trees. His body was visibly shaking.

"Are you alright?"

"I can't be with you. Not until you know a few things about me," he said through gritted teeth.

"It's ok. You can tell me." I reached for his arm before pulling away.

He turned to look at me. "I'm... I'm not sure I'm ready."

"I understand that. It's been a very long time since anyone has touched me. And when you touch me... I don't know. It's like you ignite a fire within me. You can't just leave me like this." His cock twitched in his pants. I grinned, pushing all the questions I had aside.

He stepped closer. "You ignite something within me too."

I took one last step closing the distance.

At that moment, I needed him. I would learn more about him once he satiated that need. "Please, don't stop. I need you. I'll take whatever you can give me.

"Why me?" he asked. His eyes were scrunched in fear.

"I... I don't know. My life has been full of men that are either jealous of me or are afraid of me. You are the first one in a very long time that has made me feel like a woman. Please, don't walk away."

I reached my hands out to him. His face softened as he stepped into me, wrapping his arms around me again. "We will only do what I'm ready for and nothing else?" he asked me.

"Promise."

He leaned down, kissing me and stepped a foot behind me, guiding me to the leafy bed of the forest. He laid beside me, tracing the bridge of my nose down my cheek to my lips with the tips of his fingers. Sparks spread throughout my body, adding more fuel to the fire building at my core. His touch caused more moisture to build between my legs and I was begging him to remove my pants.

"Where have you been all my life, Kassy?"

"Why do you call me Kassy? Everyone I know calls me Scarlet."

"Scarlet is your killer name. You are so much more than a Hunter." His lips were back on mine, pouring heat into my skin with every caress. His fingers trailed down my body until he found the hem of my shirt and slid between the thick fabric and my body. I sucked in a sharp breath at his touch. He brought his hand up and cupped my bare breast, massaging it with his massive fingers.

A wave of heat traveled to my core, creating new dampness. I groaned with desire for him. His tongue licked the roof of my mouth in an attempt to distract me from his hand moving southward.

I sucked in my stomach when he reached the beltline of my pants. I didn't wait for directions and raised my hips, letting him slide the pants down my ass with ease. He pulled off the boots and dragged my pants off with them before moving his hands back to my core.

I let my legs fall open as he gently stroked my clit before sliding his large finger inside. He rolled over on top of me, resting his knees on either side of mine. His desire pressed into his pants. I sat up slightly and reached out a hand to stroke the length of him. When he threw back his head and a deep rumble emanated from his chest, all the heat in my body rushed down to between my legs.

He batted my hand away and pinned me to the forest floor in a flash. His muscular arms held me down. As he pressed his body into mine, the leaves and twigs scratched my ass. I liked the pain. I wanted his whole weight to smother me.

His mouth devoured mine. He pressed his hardness into me. I wrapped my legs around his hips, pulling him tighter. His whole body vibrated against me. He lowered his lips to my neck. My desire to have him bury that scratchy beard between my thighs increased and I moaned. He kissed his way lower and lower. His teeth grazed over my hardened nipples through my shirt.

"Fuck." I groaned.

He lowered his mouth to my exposed stomach. I thought I might explode if he took any longer to hit the mark. His lips traveled lower until they finally sucked at my core. He rubbed his beard against my sensitive flesh as his tongue drank me in. I rocked against his face, begging for more.

"Please." I looked down at him.

His eyes flashed gold at my begging. His growl tore through my core, pushing me to the edge.

"Fuck me." I begged again.

Without warning he thrust two fingers into me. He worked his fingers in and out of me as his mouth nibbled at my clit.

I gripped his hair, pulling him into me. His chuckled vibrated through my core as his licks grew stronger, threatening to push me over the edge. He slid a third finger inside me as he thrust into me harder and harder. His other hand reached up and pinched at my nipple.

"Fuck, harder." I breathed and he complied.

I was shaking beneath his hold. One more thrust, and pleasure roared to the surface. My body tensed, then it released a flood of pure bliss. I had to clasp my hands over my mouth to keep from screaming out in ecstasy. My whole body shuddered as I came.

"That was...fantastic," I said after I finally took a breath again.

"And I wasn't even trying that hard." He laid down beside me and kissed my nose. "You hungry?"

"Yes," I laughed. "You want me to taste it here or to go?" I looked down at his still bulging pants.

He looked at where my eyes were still staring at and quickly covered himself with his hands.

"I meant food." He clarified.

I sat up and stroked his cheek. "But I want to return the favor." I leaned in, kissing him, and let my hand travel lower but his hand stopped me before I could get there.

"I said only what I was ready for." He pulled away from the kiss.

"Clearly, he's ready."

"Kassy," he growled.

I gave him my best pout face.

"My gods, Kassy."

"Fine. You win. Food?"

He stood first and pulled me to my feet with ease. It took me a second to find my balance, and Conri smiled when he noticed. He seemed quite proud to make my knees so weak.

I struggled to pull my pants and boots back on. He watched me the whole time, not trying to help, so I took my time making sure he saw every inch of what he did to me, even allowing my own desire to drip down my thighs.

A few minutes later, we walked back into town. As we passed the houses again, I couldn't help but wonder where the strange man beside me might live. The villages in the forest were few and far between. It was odd we had never come across each other before.

"So, where is home?" I asked him.

"I have lived just about everywhere." He pulled me into him, kissing me deeply. "I'm starving. If we don't find food soon, I might just eat you up."

I pushed the flutter in my stomach down and pulled away from him. We walked back into town to the giant tent where he purchased two bowls of stew. We devoured the food in comfortable silence before heading back to the inn. My mind kept racing back to his beard gently scratching against my thighs and the way his teeth nipped at my clit. I was getting wetter just thinking about it. But then…. Why didn't he want me to return the favor. Was I not good enough? Was it just his way of repaying me for saving his life?

I yawned as we walked, leaning into him. With one arm, he scooped me up and carried me back to the room, placing me gently on the bed.

He walked toward the door. "I'll see if they have another room yet."

I sat up quickly. "No, don't go! Please stay." I reached out for him.

Conri strolled back to the bedside, taking my hand. "I told you I can't be with you yet. It wouldn't be fair."

"I understand that. I just… I've never… No man would dare to touch me the way you do. I only want you next to me. Please?" I know I sounded desperate and afraid. Fear and I had been friends for a long time. But this was something different. Something new.

Maybe I'm clinging to this man because he isn't afraid of me?

"Does that mean you've never—."

I cut him off with a wave of my hand. "No, I have, but…." I wiped the tears from my eyes.

"But what?" He sat on the edge of the bed, stroking my cheek.

"I've only ever had one man that willingly wanted me, despite what I am. Some of the larger towns have brothels though… and I… well, let's just say it's something I'll never tell my mother about."

I couldn't read his expression as he sat there watching me.

"You…I don't understand it, but you don't look at me like I'm a freak of nature. No man has kissed me like you do… not even Nate."

Conri pulled my face to his, and gently kissed me and I sighed into him knowing it wasn't all in my head.

"I could kiss you all day," he sighed, sliding out of his boots, then pulling off mine. "Scoot over then." He grinned, and I obliged.

Laying with my back to him, enjoying the warmth of his body nuzzled against me. He draped his arm around my waist, pulling me closer. Every inch of me wanted more, but I would take whatever he would give me. The howling off in the distance didn't even stir me from his arms.

Kissing the crown of my head, Conri whispered, "Good night, Kassy."

"Good night, Conri."

9
Alone in the Woods
Conri

I waited for her breathing to slow to a steady rhythm before sliding my arm from beneath her. My body yearned for her. My pants tightened as I watched her lay there in peaceful slumber. I shoved my feet into my boots, wincing as the floorboards creaked. I looked back to where she still slept.

I'd been walking around all night with less space in my pants, and I desperately needed the release. My cock throbbed at the thought of her. I stumbled out into the forest, just out of view of any villagers that might happen by.

The soft curves of her hips flashed through my mind. I rested my left hand on the nearest tree and freed myself from my pants. I took a firm hold of my shaft, fantasizing about her warmth in my hands.

The fuck you doing? Wolfe growled in my ear.

Shut up. I barked back.

What could I be thinking? What was Wolfe thinking?

She's ours. Wolfe was screaming. *I knew it the moment I locked eyes with her. I have a right to claim her and you're out here with your dick in your hands?*

Fuck you! I won't force her!

She's a Hunter. She'd hate us forever if she finds out what we are. Wolfe had already claimed her in his mind, and I'd be lying to myself if I said I didn't want the same.

Then fucking wolf up and let me claim what's mine. Wolfe struggled for control.

No! I screamed, gripping my cock hard.

Fine! Fuck your hand then, you fucking cocksucker! Wolfe retreated but his fire blazed on. I held onto the tree to keep from walking back to that room and letting Wolfe take control.

Wolfe needed her, but this would have to suffice for now. She had to know what sleeping with me would mean for her first. I wouldn't turn her against her will. I had taken too many innocent lives into my world. She was different; it had to be her choice.

The image of her body in bed sent a wave of heat through me. I groaned as my hand traveled up my length. I closed my eyes, grasping at the picture of her body in my head. I imagined myself leaning over her, caressing her side. My hand grazed over her breast lightly. She spasmed at the feathery touch. My hand cupped her breast, and my thumb flicked over her nipple.

"Harder," she whispered to me. I obliged with a pinch, causing her to gasp. "I need you in me," she said in my mind.

I leaned over her and kissed her hungrily. My cock was so hard, I could hardly stand it. Wolfe could smell how wet she was. He begged for me to take her. My fingers caressed her slit a moment longer before I dipped just the tip of my cock inside her tight, little pussy before pulling out, then thrusting back in. She let out a tiny moan at my girth. I penetrate to the hilt, filling her.

"Conri," she gasped as I worked into her. She tightened around me, pushing me to the brink.

I slowed my thrusts, taking my time. I pulled out until only my tip remained inside of her. Dragging my hands over her stomach, I gripped her hips before stabbing back inside. I stroked her legs, bringing them up over my shoulders. Slowly, I sheathed in and out of her.

A distant howl extinguished the image of my lover. They were in the distance, but I was still too close to a Hunter for them to willingly follow me. They would kill me if they found me so vulnerable, but at this moment I didn't care. I shook the thought from my mind.

Conjuring the image of my lover back to my head, I took my shaft back in my grip. I tugged at the length, picturing her. She rolled over to her hands and knees. She turned, giving me a devious look. She shook that perfect ass at me as a giggle escaped her.

"What are you waiting for?" My hands tickled over her back. I slid my fingers around to her stomach then down to her bud as I thrusted back into her wetness.

She reached between us, clasping hard on my balls. A guttural groan escaped my lips at the image of her beneath me. I tightened my grip on her hips, pulling her into me harder and harder. She released her hold on me, gripping my thighs instead.

My breath is ragged now. The edge of release threatens me, a gloriously beautiful threat stemming from the depth of her eyes. I wanted it, craved it. How I wish I truly was between her thighs. Her tight pussy clenched around, pushing me over. I suppressed the moan that escaped my lips as I imagined my lover coming along with me.

And then the dream popped, and I was once again standing alone in the woods.

Pulling up my pants, I scanned the woods before turning my back to them. Either they hadn't sensed me, or they were leaving me be. I stood there a moment longer, gaining my composure before walking back to the inn.

I longed for a shower, but I didn't want to leave her alone for too long. Sliding into bed and wrapping my arms around her sent waves of warmth through me, threatening to excite me once again. Inhaling her cool, lavender scent, I pulled her tighter. She sighed at the pressure around her waist.

Nuzzling closer, she asked, "Where'd you go?"

"Just had to take care of something." I kissed her neck.

Her hips ground into mine. "I coulda helped." Her stomach moved with her laughter.

Wolfe growled in the back of my mind, but I pushed him back. Letting out a slow breath, I replied, "Of that I am certain, but—"

"I know. I know. You are keeping secrets." She rolled over in my arms, draping a leg over mine. She kissed me softly. "We all have our secrets. Keep yours for now, but you cannot hide them forever." She buried her face in my neck and closed her eyes.

My hands instinctively raked through her hair.

I whispered into the dark, "You are amazing, Kassy."

"I know," came her soft response.

"Kassy?"

"Hm?"

"What is it you want?" I asked.

She pulled away and stared at me in the darkness with those captivating eyes. She took me all in, studying me. I gulped down hard. A moment passed between us and I wasn't sure if she would answer.

"Bold question." She grinned.

"I have a habit of wanting things I can't have. If you're one of them, I'll leave at first light." I couldn't look her in the eyes as I spoke. I knew leaving would break me.

She pulled me closer, kissing the base of my neck. "Why define anything?" Her hands traveled down my chest, toward my stomach. Blood rushed to my member. Her lips twitched into a wicked grin as her hand stroked my cock. "Why not just have some fun for now and see what happens?"

Gasping, I pulled my hips away. "I am not just anyone, Kassy. I…." If I told her, could I beat her to her bow? "I can't." I cupped her face. "You are not just anyone, Kassy. You do not know how special you are."

Wolfe's eyes caught the tears she was trying to hide, and it was a long moment before she spoke.

"I have always just been Scarlet, the girl who likes to kill the werewolves."

"Is your friend's death the only reason you hate the wolves so much?"

"I…" She turned her face away from me and I regretted asking.

"You don't have to answer that. I'm sorry."

"No," she said, biting on her lower lip before she continued. "It's ok. I want to tell you." She looked back up at me and gave me a half-hearted smile. "I have a few to choose from. One… My grandfather, Saba, helped raise me. After my friend died, he moved out to the middle of the woods, and I rarely see him anymore. My father blamed the wolves for ruining everything—even driving his father away. I didn't…. I still don't understand, but my father wouldn't let me see my Saba after that." She turned her face away and half whispered. "I snuck out to visit him anyway."

"And the other?"

She shifted uncomfortably. "I…" I moved my hand, so our pinkies touched. She shivered. "A…friend…was killed on my first hunt." She looked up at me. "Can we just leave it at that?"

I knew this friend was more than a friend, and it took all my strength to keep Wolfe from clawing his way to the surface, so I could only nod at her.

"The wolves have taken everything I ever loved. If…." She wiped the tears from her cheeks. "If it weren't for the wolves, I'd have my best friend, my Saba, and…and Nate. My father changed after Rose, almost as much as I did. He said some pretty awful things about his father."

Wolfe roared at hearing another man's name spill from her lips but I held perfectly still as I asked, "And your mother?"

She scoffed. "All my mother has ever cared about is getting me married off. She doesn't understand."

"Understand what?"

"That I don't really care about marriage."

I reminded myself that marriage amongst the wolves differed greatly from with the humans. We mate for love and life, not out of necessity. Still, my stomach turned as images of her marrying another man, any man, filled my mind. I had to wonder if she was entirely against settling down with just one man or if it was just the modern notion of marriage she was against.

I had to gather my courage to ask, "Why?"

She laughed. "My parents hate each other. What good is marriage when there is no love?"

"And what about love?"

"I have to pay for love. So, is there really such a thing? You always pay for love in the end, so why bother?"

Pulling her closer, I whispered, "Love and sex are not mutually exclusive. I am sure you are amazing in bed but you can still fall in love without sex." She looked up at me and I grinned wickedly. "Although I do hope to find out someday just how amazing you are, but for now, this is enough." I squeezed her tight.

Her smile didn't quite reach her eyes. "For how long? How long could you withstand your desires?"

"First, it's been far too long since someone else handled my desire, so I can wait. And second, if someone would keep her hands off me, I would be more inclined to withstand any need." She pouted her lips, begging me to press mine into them. "You're killing me, Kassy!" Tilting my head down to hers, I gave into my desire just a little. She was warm against my lips. My cock stiffened at her hands against my abs and Wolfe came bubbling to the surface. I pushed her back down to the bed pinning her in place. My kisses grew rougher with each passing second. Her hand slipped between the cloth of my pants and grazed the tip of my cock before I gained control over Wolfe.

Pulling away, I grasped her hand. "Kassy…." I breathed.

"I'm sorry. I know you're trying." She looked away but the grin she hid told me she wasn't all that sorry.

"It's…" I sighed. I pushed off the bed and walked to the window. The moon wasn't full yet but the pull of the change called to me and I knew the longer we lingered here the harder it would be to hide our true nature. Her soft hand on my arm jolted me from my thoughts and back to the conversation at hand. "It's just that sex with me is different from any other guy you might have been with." I brushed my hand over her face. "If I were to have sex with you, I could hurt you."

"Aha. Cocky much?" Her eyes traveled to the bulge in my pants.

"No. It's not like that." I laughed. "Well, maybe a little, but that's not what I mean." I pushed the curtains aside and stared aimlessly out the window. It might have just been my imagination, but I thought I saw through the flimsy fabric two eyes flash at the edge of the forest.

"Hey." She crawled from the bed to stand beside me.

I looked at her for just a second, but when I turned back toward the window, the eyes didn't appear again.

"I was just messing with you," she said.

Draping an arm around her, I pressed my lips into her crown.

"It's not an easy thing, this... issue of mine. If I tell you, it'll change everything." I pulled her tighter. "I can't explain to you why, but I can't ruin this."

She wrapped her arms around my waist, resting her cheek on my bare chest. "Then don't. Tell me when you are ready. I will do my best to stop teasing you."

I smiled. "You could only do that if you could erase yourself from my memory."

She punched me in the gut playfully. "Let's go back to sleep, then."

10
Shooting Lessons
Scarlet

The first rays of sunlight peered through the sheer curtains. I never thought I'd be one to be happy to wake up next to someone, but today I was. Even with the quiet growling noises he was making. I knew this man would only lead to trouble, but at this moment I didn't care. Being near him made my soul happy, and in this world we get few opportunities to be truly happy, and I'd take mine when I could.

I rolled over, his arm still draped over me, and brushed his long hair from his face. Running my fingertips across his brow and down the bridge of his nose calmed the sounds he was making.

He sighed, pulling me tighter against his chest. My heart fluttered at being so close to him. I nuzzled against his chest and listened to the slow, rhythmic beat of his heart.

"Morning," he said without opening his eyes. I smiled as his words rumbled through me.

"Morning. You know you make some strange noises when you sleep?" We lay there in peaceful silence a long moment before he responded.

"I have been told that before. Sorry. Did I wake you?" He leaned in and kissed my forehead. Warmth spread down to my toes.

"Yeah, but it was kinda cute, so it's okay." I stole a quick kiss from his lips. The corner of his mouth curled upward and I had to resist kissing them longer.

"So, what do you want to do today?" he asked, finally opening his eyes.

I buried my head in his chest and inhaled deeply. He smelled of petrichor, reminding me of the woods after a spring storm.

"This," I said. I purred as he stroked my back. "I could stay here forever." I breathed him in and his body tensed under mine, but he made no attempt to extricate himself from me.

"What about the hunt?"

"It's still early in the hunt," I said, even though he was right. My funds were running low, but I didn't want to let go of him. He leaned back and raised my chin so that my eyes met his.

"Hunting is your only source of income. I won't let you go hungry." His eyes hardened.

"Ugh." I pulled him closer, gently kissing his lips but this time he did not budge and kiss me back. "Fine then. How about this? You are a terrible shot. If I teach you to shoot, you can help me on my hunt once your shoulder heals. Think of this as your way to pay me back for saving your life." I hovered over his lips taunting him. "How's that sound?"

"Sounds…interesting." His eyes traveled to my lips still so close to his before he looked back at my eyes. He tilted his head, avoiding my lips, and instead he kissed my nose and slid out from under me. I rolled over with a groan. His chuckle sent me into a frenzy, and I chucked a pillow at his head which he dodged easily. "Play nice, Kassy."

"I don't like fighting fair." I said.

He sighed and turned his back to me before slowly and carefully getting up out of bed.

Standing to his full height in this room proved difficult for him. "Let's go then." He yanked on his boots and tossed me mine. I sat up and pulled them on while still in the bed and slowly climbed out. I grabbed my cloak, pack, and crossbow from the chair and headed to the door.

We stopped in the small dining room to pick up some bread. The small, rickety table was full of travelers from the fair. Their clothing looked strange compared to that of the townsfolk. I hadn't noticed them before but now they stood out. The townsfolk tended to have lighter clothing whereas the fair workers all wore black and spoke in a language I couldn't understand. Not one person looked at Conri as he stepped into the small space, grabbed a loaf of bread, and led me into the cool morning air.

"I'm more of a meat-eater than a bread guy," he informed me, closing the door behind us.

Bumping into him in the thigh with my hip, I replied with a grin, "More motivation for you to learn how to shoot then."

His powerful arms wrapped around my middle, pulling my back against his chest. My spine vibrated with the growl that resonated from deep in the pit of his stomach. My heart quickened. *Where was this Conri ten minutes ago?* The desire to drag him back to our room was so strong, I had to keep teasing.

"Maybe we can find you a cute little bunny rabbit. They are delicious." I rubbed my ass against him. Clearly, food was the last thing on his mind.

His hands intertwined with my hair as he pulled my head to one side. "I could devour you." His fiery breath on my neck made my body tense against his. His lips gently kissed the flesh behind my ear. All my strength evaporated, and I'd do whatever this man wanted, even right here for all to see. "But we really should go." He relaxed his grip on me. My hopes of something more deflated.

His face strained as I reached for it, but he caught my wrist before I could touch him. "Where are we going?" he asked through gritted teeth.

"Are you…" I opened my mouth to ask, but his stern face told me not to ask what was wrong. "There's a range on the edge of the village. I thought we'd start there," I said with a neutral tone.

We walked in silence past the small houses and reached the range quickly. On the far end, the townsfolk had placed round targets in front of a wooden wall. Thin ropes stretched back to where we stood and were tied to poles, separating each target. I placed my pack and bow on the small table at the end of one row.

Conri stared off into nothing as his skin turned a slight shade of green. "Are you okay?" I asked, but he didn't even flinch when I spoke. Touching his shoulder, I asked again, "Are you okay, Conri?"

"Yeah." He turned to look at me, his eyes distant.

"We don't have to do this. I didn't even think about the fact that you were just shot. Is that what's bugging you?" I gently grazed his wounded shoulder.

"It's fine, really. Wherever you are is where I want to be." He grabbed my hand and brought it to his lips. "I promise."

My cheeks flushed, and I had to pull away. This man was a walking contradiction. One minute he was pinning me against him and the next he was straight faced. I needed my own head to be clear if I wanted to teach him to hunt. I walked over, picked up my crossbow, and handed it to him. The wooden stock made it sturdy, but the recurve of the bow made pulling the string harder.

"This loop on the top is the stirrup. You place it on the ground and stick your foot in it and pull up on the string until you hear it click into place. Try it."

I watched as Conri wiggled his enormous foot into the stirrup. The toe of his boot simply would not fit. He pulled on the string, but it slipped from his hands several times. I stepped back, giving him space. After the third attempt failed, I had to cover my face to hide my grin. He tried. Bless him, he tried. Even though he outweighed me tenfold, he couldn't do it. I couldn't stop myself as I burst into a fit of laughter.

"What?" He snapped.

"I... I'm sorry." I gasped. "I couldn't help it." I squatted down and pulled my goat's foot lever from my pack, hoping he wouldn't be offended when I offered him this apparatus for bending the crossbow. "Even for a vigorous man like you, my bow is pretty difficult to cock by hand. Try the lever." Not looking him in the eye, I showed him how to attach the metal lever to the strings on the crossbow. He didn't say a word. When I finally looked up, his eyes traveled up and down me as if he were picturing my body beneath my clothes. He licked his lips, and a small growl escaped him. I gulped hard and tried to ignore the shiver that ran down my spine.

He cocked the crossbow and I handed him a bolt. "Place this in the groove, one fletching down. Make sure the nock is sitting in the string." To my surprise, he was good at taking directions. Most men hated when a woman told them what to do. I was an expert with my bow but every year, a new recruit refused to listen to me and ended up hurting himself or the bow. "Okay, now step over here and aim. You are stronger than I am, so it'll be easier for you to hold the crossbow straight. That target is pretty far, so aim a little higher than where you want to hit."

He lifted an eyebrow at me. "Why do you use this crossbow anyway? Aren't there lighter weapons you could use?"

"Yes, I could, but this was my Saba's. I've grown accustomed to its weight."

His face turned sour as he raised the bow.

I stepped up next to him and guided his hands. "Tilt your head so you are looking down the shaft of the arrow. Line it up to where you want to hit, then raise it a little. Once you're ready, pull the trigger." I stepped to the side to watch. "Oh, and breathe."

He did just what I said, and the bolt stuck a little left of center. Not even a seasoned vet, trained with a sword, would have followed my instructions so well. He continued to hold the bow in place a moment after the arrow hit the target before he lowered to the table.

"I'm impressed. Few can do that on their first try. Do you want to keep practicing, or do you want to go find us a rabbit?"

"I'm hungry. If you're going to make me kill and clean my own food, then let's go find something," he grumbled.

"You're cranky when you're hungry, aren't you?" I laughed, pulling myself up on my toes to kiss his nose.

He grabbed my arms and lifted me to the table's edge. Hunger burned in his eyes. With his knee, he spread my legs, stepping between them. I begged him with my eyes. He hesitated before bringing his lips closer. I wrapped my legs around his hips and pulled him against me. His eyes closed as he nuzzled his lips to my neck. My skin tingled as his beard brushed against me, sending tremors throughout my body.

"I need to eat before something bad happens," he whispered.

Reaching my hands under his shirt placing them against his bare chest, I replied, "Bad can be good."

He growled in response, and my body ached to give in to every desire I had.

"Kassy—" He pulled my hands away and untangled himself from my legs before stepping back. "Not like this."

"Hey, wait." I pulled him closer, placing my palms on either side of his broad face. "You started this..." His cheeks burned under my touch. "I don't understand what you want from me and I..."

With a shudder, he walked out of reach, back toward the road. His warmth disappeared, and a chill settled over me as he disappeared from view, leaving me behind with only my crossbow for company.

11
A Peak into the Past
Conri

*H*er aroma lingered on my skin as I walked away. Wolfe screamed at me for not taking her then and there. Kassy was a Hunter, though. If Wolfe took her without her knowing the truth, the forced bond might kill us all.

I needed food. Fresh, red meat. I headed toward the woods, my stomach churning as I recalled the unfamiliar bow in my hands. I couldn't breathe and thought I might puke all at the same time. I hit my knees. As I grabbed and pulled fistfuls of my hair, pulling at the roots in my scalp.

I hadn't lost control of Wolfe in decades, but I was on the brink now. Involuntary tears fell from my eyes. Every muscle ached from the need to shift. The need to feed. The need to have her under me.

I needed to protect her from Wolfe, even if that meant leaving. I stood on shaky legs without looking back. I'd walk out into those trees and straight to the pack that hunted me.

"Hey."

I jolted at her soft voice before it washed over me, calming my fears.

"I can't." I choked out.

Her voice stopped me before I could take more than a single step. "Wait." Desperation pleaded in her voice. "Don't go."

Hints of salt fluttered through her lavender scent. Turning my head just enough to peer over her face sent waves of pain through my chest.

Her wet cheeks and red and puffy eyes stabbed through me like a dagger. I couldn't stand to see the pain I'd caused her. Looking back toward the trees ahead, I tried to steady my breath. I clamped my hands into tight fists.

"Kassy, you deserve someone who won't lie to you."

"What have you lied about?"

"Myself."

"What lies have you told me?"

"I...well, I guess I haven't directly lied to you, but...."

"Then you haven't lied to me."

"But you don't really know me. Not the truth of me."

"Where were you born?" She glided into view in front of me and sat with her back to the forest. Those green eyes gazed up at me.

"The forest. I know it sounds odd, but that's the truth." A sense of relief flooded over me. At least I had told her one truthful thing.

She reached out her hand, weaving her strong fingers between mine.

"Sit with me? Talk with me? You know so much about me. Can I ask you more questions before you run away?"

I gave her a curt nod, and she continued. "What about your family? Your parents?"

Sitting on the cold, hard ground in front of her, I laughed. "I have a large family. And an even larger extended family. My parents died several winters ago."

Kassy hesitated a moment before she leaned forward, and her soft hand squeezed mine. "I'm sorry."

"I come from a long line of nomads. We move around a lot. One winter we came across a pack of wild dire cats." I shook the memory out of my head. "My father led our warriors, giving the rest of the clan time to run." I studied the leaves and the dirt before me, remembering the roars of the massive cats and the growls of my father's wolf. "We ran and ran, but he never came back." Kassy inched closer to me, and I looked her in the eyes. I wanted to throw up a wall and put as much distance between her and I as I could. I also wanted to smash all my walls and tell this woman everything.

"The following winter, my mom passed. My little brother was playing on the ice and fell through. She jumped in to save him and got stuck under the ice."

Kassy sat up on her knees and pulled me into a hug before saying, "I am so sorry." I breathed her in for a moment before releasing her from the embrace. Getting these things off my chest and telling her gave me a moment of peace. Even if they were only half truths, telling her felt right.

"That's not the worst of it. My older brother challenged our leader and didn't survive."

"My gods. What kind of leader do you have?" She was tearing through my walls like fire. The death of my brother was by far the worst possible memory I had, but I was sharing it with her. She had no idea what she was getting into. She had no idea of the avalanche she had started. How could I possibly tell her this leader I speak of was me?

I scoffed. "A vicious one." I wiped the moisture from my face. "He left recently, and an even worse leader took his place."

"Is that why you left?"

"Sorta." I looked her in the eyes looking for some sign I could trust her with everything. "I'm still not telling you the whole truth. I can't. It'll hurt too much."

She stroked my face. "I'm sorry. I don't mean to upset you. You can stop."

I took her hand in mine and brought it to my lips, kissing her softly. "I don't mind. When my mother died, she left me in charge of my siblings. I am the oldest of nine. The youngest was fourteen when mother died."

"Nine children? Dang, your mom must have been amazing." Kassy stared at me. Her face was full of admiration, which warmed my heart. Memories of my mother washed over me.

"She was incredible." I drifted off, remembering all the times my mother had been there for me. And how much I missed her now.

Kassy cupped the nape of my neck. Her gentle fingers entwined in my hair. She pulled me to her, kissing me deeply. My heart raced at her touch.

She pulled away slightly, whispering in my ear, "And what of past lovers?"

I laughed. "Lovers? I have had plenty of sex, but very few lovers." She cocked her head at me. "My clan doesn't take love lightly, so when we take a lover, it's more than just a passing fling. We enjoy sex as much as anyone, but sex for the release is different from sex for love."

"Have you had lovers then?"

"I…I've had a few. Only one that really mattered to me."

Her fingers traced the outline of my lips.

"What happened to her? Where is she now?" she asked.

I met her eyes. "You are asking all the hard questions, aren't you?"

She pressed her lips back to mine with tantalizing quickness. A look of mischief was on her brow.

"She…she's dead as well."

Kassy pulled away, clasping her hands over her mouth. Her shoulders slumped, and the humor immediately drained from her face.

"I'm so sorry." She said through her hands. She placed her hand tenderly on my knee. "I really am stepping into it. You don't have to answer any more."

I cupped her face in my hand. "No, I want to. Damn, Kassy, but you make me want to confess everything to you, too." I stared into those eyes a moment before I continued. "Her name was Abrielle. She was gentle and wise, but a jealous member of my clan killed her. He wanted her but couldn't have her. He hated me for all I had, and he wanted to hurt me." Her image came flooding back to me, nearly breaking me in two. I remembered her moving like water through a stream.

Her dark hair blended so well into the nights sky, she practically disappeared.

"What happened to him?" Kassy's question broke me from the memory.

"Let's just say that when I caught up to him, he didn't see the next moon rise. I made him pay for every moment of pain and worry he had caused her. I didn't even leave enough of him for the birds."

Silence settled between us. I expected her to run at my sudden confession. The truth was that what I had done was brutal. I had allowed Wolfe complete control that night. To my surprise, Kassy didn't stand. She didn't make a single move to flee.

"He got what he deserved."

That one sentence nearly broke me. The fact that this stunning woman in front of me looked at me without judgment was nothing short of a miracle. A miracle I didn't deserve.

"Things went a little dark for me after that. I honestly can't remember much of the next several winters."

Kassy nodded again, as if she understood.

The rumble of my stomach broke the long silence that followed.

Kassy stood, picking up her bow and reaching for me. "Thank you for sharing a part of your life with me. I am sorry it hurt so much."

I gripped her arm as I stood. A great weight had been lifted from me.

She handed me the bow, and the light had returned to her eyes. "Wanna kill something?" My stomach did flips as I studied her face for a moment.

I took the bow from her, and we headed for the trees.

12
The Hunt
Scarlet

$\mathcal{I}$nterlacing his fingers with mine, we walked deeper into the woods. A comfortable silence settled around us, and we walked until the trees were so thick that they obscured the sun above us. As we followed the game trail through the forest, Conri took the lead. For once, I was happy to follow.

We walked for several minutes, and I found myself mesmerized by his fluid grace. More than once, I let my mind wander as I stared at the way his leather pants cupped his firm ass. I imagined again what it would be like to see those pants on the floor of the inn, or even the brush at our feet.

I nearly slammed into him when he stopped abruptly. He twisted his head to his left. I stared in the direction he was looking but saw nothing. He lifted a finger to his lips and grabbed my pack, pulling out the lever and an arrow from my quiver. He cocked and loaded it before stepping off the path and into the brush.

"Hey! Wait a second," I started before he glared at me to be silent. "I don't see anything," I whispered.

He turned and tapped his ear and pointed back in the direction he was walking. I hesitated a moment before shrugging my shoulders. I continued to follow him. We walked and walked before I finally saw it. She stood a hundred yards in front of us.

"A deer?" I hissed. Even a small doe could feed a family for weeks. "That's too much meat."

He ignored my protests and took his aim. The beautiful doe bowed her head, completely unaware of our presence. Conri pulled the trigger. The arrow struck her just behind her front leg, and she dropped where she stood. Anger boiled inside me, and my fist connected with his lower back.

"What the hell? That is far too much meat for the two of us! This is a total waste!"

"You've not seen me eat. And besides what we don't eat, we can give to the inn. I'm sure they need the meat."

"And let me guess. You don't know how to gut a deer?" I spat.

"Never have done it myself," he said, grinning at me.

"Fine." I shoved him out of the way, unsheathing my knife. I made quick work with my blade, skillfully cutting through the hide down to the muscle. I opened her up and pulled out everything that wasn't edible and saved everything that was. The warmth of her chased away the cool air and fueled my anger.

"There. Now, you get to carry her back. Take her to the butcher in town. What we don't use, we can sell." I stormed off back the way we had come, bloody hands and all. We took our kill straight to the shop. I gave Conri the meat I harvested and made my way to the bathhouse to clean up.

The hot water cooled my temper as I stood, washing my skin clean. Once again, a less experienced Hunter refused to listen and did his own thing.

I stomped back to the inn and slammed the door behind me. The anger completely vanished once I smelled the freshly cooked meat.

Conri stepped into the little dining room with two plates of steaming food and a lilac apron wrapped around his chest. He set the plates down on the table closest to me, under the one window in the room.

"The butcher said he'd have the meat back to us at the end of the day. He'd normally let the meat age for several days, but I told him we needed it sooner. The cook was busy, so I hope you don't mind, but I went ahead and cooked what we had."

"What are you wearing?" I asked, as I clutched at my stomach with laughter.

"It's all the innkeeper had." He tore it off and threw it at my chest. A sour look crossed his face. "Do you want the food or not?" The tiny wooden chair squeaked in protest as he pulled it out roughly, waiting for me to sit.

"Yes." I sat. After a moment, he sat beside me. "I'm sorry I got angry with you. Thank you for the food." I leaned in, kissing his cheek before taking my first bite. Hunting with my Saba had been the last time I'd had venison. Every bite melted in my mouth.

"How did you learn to track so well?" I interrupted his chewing.

He swallowed hard before answering. "I have always had a keen sense of hearing. I heard a noise and just followed it."

I dropped my fork and stared at him. He was lying to me... or rather, holding back the truth. I couldn't pinpoint it, but something about his words was off.

"I didn't hear a thing. And I'm a pretty good Hunter." I couldn't keep the skepticism from my voice.

Conri shrugged, taking another bite. My irritation resurfaced. After all he had shared in the woods, why would he not share something as simple as who had taught him to hunt?

We finished our meal in silence. I was so hungry that I'd leave the fight until later. I wasn't about to drop the conversation, but my stomach still rumbled for more. When I ate my fill, I looked at him, fully bracing for an argument, but his lustful eyes sent a shiver down my spine.

"What?" I asked, mildly frustrated.

"Watching you today." He licked his lips in a slow and deliberate manner. "The way you spoke to me. No one has ever gotten mad at me like that." His hand cupped the nape of my neck, pulling me across the table and closer to him. "It's pretty sexy." He kissed my neck lingering there for a long moment causing my heart to stop, "Let's go upstairs," he whispered in my ear.

Conri stood, pulling me to my feet. We had barely made halfway up the dark stairwell before he pinned my back against his chest. His hands tightened on my hips, pulling me into him. Blood pumped faster and faster. I reached around gripping his hips.

His breath was hot against my neck as his lips trailed lower down my spine. One hand climbed up under my shirt brushing the bottom of my breast as the other traveled down over my belly button.

Faint candlelight flickered at the top of the staircase. I waited for someone to discover us, and the danger only made my longing worse. I needed him now and I didn't care who saw.

Conri's rough thumb rubbed at my nipple while his other hand traveled under the hem of my pants. I moved my feet apart giving him clear access and leaned into him. His fingers teased at my wetness pulling a moan from my lips. He growled in response.

"Conri." I breathed, out begging for more.

"Kassy," he rasped.

I gasped as he plunged one finger inside while his thumb circled my clit. I rocked to the rhythm of his thrust. I laid my head on his shoulder, gripped the base of his neck wishing I could devour him.

He pulled away from the kiss. "I want to taste you on my tongue." He breathed into my ear. His arm wrapped around my middle, fingers still toying with my core, lifted me off the steps and carried me to our room.

The second we were behind a closed door, Conri threw me down on the bed and crawled toward me like a wild animal about to devour his prey. Pinning my arms above my head, he pressed his hard body against mine. I ground my hips against his hardened cock.

With his free hand, he tore through my shirt, exposing my breasts. He released my arms, and I let them hang over the edge of the bed as he placed all his weight on my hips. This man was all mine and I'd let him take what he needed from me tonight. He glided his fingertips from my neck to my navel. I thought my pants would catch fire for the heat building within them.

He lowered his body to the end of the bed, trailing rough kisses and bites along the way until he knelt to the floor and pulled my boots and pants off with haste. My legs fell open, exposing me completely to him. Moisture seeped into the sheets. He straightened, pressing his hips into mine. I rubbed my wet pussy against his pants, groaning at the stiffness of his cock.

His eyes burned with desire. "I am going to eat you up." He plunged his tongue roughly into my mouth while his hands reached between us and found my clit. His fingers twirled around it, sending sparks through me. My cunt ached to welcome his girth.

Gasping, I begged, "Please, don't tease."

"I make the rules, remember?" he grinned, as he slid down my body until he knelt on the floor. He yanked my legs toward him, so my ass found the edge of the bed. Slowly, he slid two fingers inside me and rubbed my clit with his thumb. *Faster. Harder.* I demanded in my head and as if he heard me he slammed his fingers inside me over and over.

I had to throw a pillow over my face to keep from screaming. I was so close to the edge.

His grin was positively wicked as he pulled one finger and then another out of my core.

"Fuck!" I yelled at him.

He stuck his fingers in his mouth, and a new flood of heat built my center.

"You taste delicious." He lowered his face, licking the lips between my thighs. He slid his fingers back to my core and rubbed slow circles inside me. His mouth worked its way up to my core, sucking hard as his fingers moved with increasing intensity. "I want you to come for me." He breathed against me before his tongue resumed its licking.

"Fu...fu...fuck!" I screamed into the pillow as a wave of pleasure flooded me. My orgasm only fueled the fire that burned inside me and only his cock with quench it.

I grabbed his collar and pulled him back to the bed. My hands quickly found the buckle of his pants and had them down his ass before either of us could change our mind. A look of surprise passed over him, but he didn't stop me. Fire burned the confusion from his face as I wrapped my legs around his bare hips and pulled him to me. The tip of his shaft glistened just as ready for this moment as I was. I pressed his hard cock against my clit. He moaned as he pressed into me harder.

"I want you so much. Right now." I gripped his ass, grinding my pussy against his cock. I continued to move against him. "Do you want me as much?"

He leaned down, kissing me. His breath was coming in quick bursts now. His hands pulled at the ends of my hair, but I didn't mind. His enormous cock sent chills down my spine. It was so close to penetrating me that all I'd have to do was shift slightly and it would slide right in. I thrust my hips up rocking my wet pussy against his cock, lining the two up.

"Is that a yes?" I moved my hand, gripping his shaft, sliding his head in my slickness.

Conri froze. His entire body stiffened, and his eyes went wide and he broke out in a cold sweat. The look on his face reminded me of the night we met. Even his arms vibrated before something finally broke him from his hold, and he shook his head.

I barely had time to process what was happening, as he jumped off the bed like it was on fire. He yanked his pants up as he hurried toward the door.

"I...I can't," he stuttered. Without another word, he closed the door behind him.

13
The Wolf
Conri

Staggering out of the inn, I ran toward the tree line. I turned back and gazed up at the small window of our room. I had to leave her. A connection I'd detected with her was stronger than any other creature I'd ever encountered, but changing her without her knowledge would kill her. Steeling my resolve, I dove deeper into the woods.

My muscles burned with every step. She would be safer without me. She would get over the pain of this soon enough and go on to live a normal human life and I'd find a way to survive. But Wolfe fought me to turn back. He wanted to ravage her on that tiny bed. I ignored the desire to do the same. Blood pulsed inside my ears, drowning out all sounds. I wrapped my arms around a tree, the bark biting into my palms, stopping Wolfe from walking back.

Pulling myself away from the tree, I kept walking. Wolfe kept fighting to take control, and if he won, I had to be as far from Kassy as possible. I headed for a small, grassy knoll. I paced in the grass, walking between the trees. Wolfe wanted to stay. I needed to run.

My vision turned red as I slammed my fist straight through a tree. Another, softer sound echoed in the quiet forest. I turned around quickly, snapping my head back and looking for the source of the noise. When I saw nothing but the trees and heard small prey, I resumed my pacing.

"You cannot win. I won't let you take her," I shouted out loud. But yelling at Wolfe only made him fight harder. Pain seared through me as gravity pulled me to my knees. "No!" I demanded, trying to stand. My body shook from the struggle. "Please, no," I begged.

My muscles burned as they grew to twice their size, tearing my clothes from my body. My eyes, wet with tears, looked at the sky. My jaw clamped down at the anguish as my joints twisted. Blood dripped from my mouth as fangs protruded from my lips. My naked skin grew a shiny fur coat.

Wolfe had won.

He howled at his victory while my small voice whimpered in defeat. The noise I thought I heard turned into a crash, and our eyes quickly found the intruder scrambling to stand back up.

Kassy scrambled to her feet not even an arm's length away from us. Recognition and fear flashed across her face.

A lifetime past in mere moments and I saw the potential life I could have with her and it didn't frighten me nearly as much as I thought it would. We would never be alone if she chose us over the Hunt.

Wolfe had chosen her. I knew he wouldn't hurt her, but what he did surprised even me. He lowered his head and bowed deeply toward her in submission, a sign of respect rarely granted our kind, especially from Wolfe.

Kassy stood and her head cocked to one side. For a brief moment, her eyes studied us and we wondered if it was the last time we'd gaze upon her. She reached out her hand as if in goodbye before turning to run. The forest engulfed her tiny from in seconds and we were alone again.

Suppressing the desire to run after her, we lowered the rest of our body to the ground. Kassy had seen us naked and exposed. She knew everything we were, and she ran. She had defeated me as wholly as Wolfe had. We lay on the hard earth until the cold seeped into our soul.

Pain stabbed at our chest, constricting our breathing. Every bone in our body, every strand of fur screamed exactly what we had known from that first day she had rescued us in the forest. She was not just a lover, but our mate. Our true mate. Wolfe could smell it in her before we even laid eyes on her. But she was human, and I was the Sage, and no wolf had ever been mated to a human. Standing here alone and broken, I knew the truth.

I reached out for Wolfe, needing his rage, but he was silent. Kassy had broken the monster within and left us hollow.

I had loved Abrielle, but what I held for Kassy was unlike anything I'd ever known. My heart had broken when Abrielle died, but at this moment, the rejection from my true mate might actually kill me.

My insides boiled with each memory of Kassy begging for the truth while I pushed her away. I should never have ran toward her but let the Silver Silence finish the job. I should have died that day and not ruined both our lives. Kassy was the only one I would ever love, no matter how long I lived. Even if I couldn't have her, I'd always belong to her. I had waited three-hundred winters to find her, and I had broken her. I had broken both of us.

I would have gladly laid there until death came calling but Wolfe refused to give up so easily. He pushed me into action. I forced our feet to walk to the edge of the forest where the village came into view. In the distance, we saw the little inn. Sniffing the air, we could tell she was still inside, and we pictured her asleep on the pillow, or worse, crying into it all alone.

We paced the forest floor wondering our next move.

How can we convince her to believe us? I asked Wolfe.

I could have taken her. Wolfe finally spoke with venom in his voice.

I know but…

Yes… Not against her will. I get it. But now look at us. That bitch is breaking us.

But we love her.

Fuck you! I know that! She is my mate, and you wouldn't let me handle it then, so why are you asking for my opinion now? If left to me, I'd hunt her down and fuck her right now. Wolfe barked.

No! I screamed. *Fine! I'll try to stop her!*

Fucking pussy. Wolfe growled.

I ignored him and walked along the forest's edge until we came closer to the inn. The smell of horses filled our nose as we neared the stables.

Kassy's scent moved from the inn to the barn. The tangy citrus mixed with that intoxicating lavender smell stopped us in our tracks. We sat in between the trees, unable to see her but knew she was close.

Our wolf ears picked up the fight she was having with the stable boy and we knew she was preparing to leave.

We'll lose her if we do nothing. Wolfe's voice came out in a high pitched panic. I had to work to steady my breathing.

She'll run faster if she sees you! I barked back.

Wolfe stubbornly held onto control of our body.

What are you going to do to convince her to stay, Wolfe? Are you really going to rape our mate?

Wolfe shrank back to the depths of our mind and my body contorted and shifted back to my human form. I lay in the mud, breathless for a moment. Forcing myself to stand, I followed her scent. She would have to walk right past me before leaving town. This was my last chance to explain to her. I had to try.

Stepping out of the cover of the trees, I stood naked and more than a little afraid to lose her. Wolfe had wanted her. He had needed her on some primal level that was hard to fight. But even more, I was in love with her. She was my soul. Her horse trotted toward me.

"Kassy," I whispered too afraid of seeing her reject us again. "Kassy!" I found my voice and shouted for her.

Her heart rate increased at the sound of my voice and I knew she heard me but she didn't flinch. "Please, Kassy! Stay! I need to explain!" I begged her, but she merely nudged her horse into a gallop. I watched her go until I could no longer see her. My heart shattered.

I darted back into the woods and shifted painfully quick back into Wolfe. He howled a mournful song before sprinting into the darkness.

Scarlet

My boot connected with the door as he ran through it. What was his deal, anyway? He toyed with me, but won't follow through. I knew he was hiding something, but damn.

Fuck it. I won't let him get away with this.

Jumping out of bed, I got dressed as fast as I could and headed out of the inn. A path of upturned tables and stalls led in the direction of the forest. After that, I listened for the sounds of branches and underbrush being trampled.

Awe filled me as I stared at the trail of broken branches that followed in his wake. I knew he was strong, but to rip limbs clear from trees?

A deep howl came from the direction he had gone. Reaching for my bow, I remembered I had once again left it in the room.

"Damn." I didn't even have a knife.

I crouched low and walked slowly toward the sound. Wiping my damp palms on my pants, I took a deep breath, trying to control my racing heart.

I eased my way to the edge of the small clearing. I knelt behind a tree and watched Conri pace. His massive form overshadoweded the among the saplings. He huffed as he stomped from tree to tree, stopping in front of a tree that was bigger around than my hips. I clasped a hand over my mouth to keep from yelping when his fist slammed clean through the trunk, sending the tree crashing down.

I fell to my ass and scrambled backwards.

What was he? I'd never seen a man—or beast, for that matter—take out a tree like that. My instincts screamed at me to run, but I was frozen in place.

His entire body tightened, and his breathing grew ragged. A rumble seemed to emanate from him, filling the small clearing with its sound.

"No!" He clenched his teeth.

He spun around like some force had shoved him backwards. The ground shook when he dropped to one knee. It was like an invisible hand had pulled him to the ground. A deep growl echoed around me. Arching his back, Conri whimpered in pain.

Tears fell from his now golden eyes as he whispered, "No more."

Despite my terror, I ached to soothe him.

What was happening?

I watched in horror as his body grew larger, wider, as his limbs grew longer and tore through his clothes, leaving him naked. At the sound of his bones cracking, my dinner threatened to spill from me. I held back a scream as his body twisted at odd angles.

Those beautiful lips that had rubbed against mine so gently disappeared. His head grew longer, and his teeth elongated into fangs just before his skin sprouted fur.

He's a wolf. I was trembling. *He can't be a wolf. Werewolves are frozen in wolf form.* Was everything I knew a lie? I had to be seeing things. This wasn't happening.

Things Conri had said and done finally clicked into place. The silver in his back nearly killed him but once it was out he was stronger than any man I'd ever known. His unwillingness to sleep with me yet his burning desire to do just that. Everything now made sense.

As if confirming my fears, the wolf sat on his haunches and howled. Then he lowered his head with a whimper.

The ice in my veins melted away, and I stood quickly and turned, crashing through the small trees. I had to try to outrun him. His eyes snapped to mine, but he didn't move. He cocked his head when our eyes met, and I froze.

As a wolf, he was even more massive. I had been taught all my life that werewolves were beasts. But he was beautiful. His golden eyes held me transfixed as if looking into the surface of the sun. His dark coat was as black as the night sky over his spine and ears, but his face, legs, and underbelly showed a gorgeous mix of salt and pepper.

He moved one foot forward and lowered his head so his nose touched the forest floor.

Is he bowing to me?

I had to run before he raised his head. But I couldn't move. He sat up again and cocked his head at me, waiting. Waiting for me to bow back? For me to submit? To surrender?

"I... I..." Tears streamed down my face as I turned my back to him. I ran before I could change my mind. Branches smacked my face, shooting pain through me. But I kept running. I didn't stop until I reached my room where his scent lingered.

I froze with thoughts of him. The way his hands held me so gently. How his body fit perfectly against mine. How his scent welcomed me home. But he was a wolf. Wolves only took. My hands shook as I looked down and only saw blood... Nate's blood. His shredded body, cold and forever frozen in the woods. The memory of the weight of the knife in my hand as I plunged it into the face of his attacker finally made my decision for me.

I threw all my things in my pack and over my shoulder and bolted back to the front desk.

"Here's what I owe you. I need my horse. Now!" I snapped at the girl.

"I'll get the stable boy to saddle him."

"No. I'll do it. I need to leave right now. If my...companion comes back, don't tell him anything." I stormed out of the door and ran around to the stables.

I grabbed Jericho's bridle and threw it on, jumping on bareback. The stable boy's eyes were wide with fear as he jumped out of my way. I trotted toward the door without so much as apologizing to him.

"I can have him saddled in a few minutes for you if you want," he yelled at me.

"No. Keep the saddle. Or sell it. I don't care. I need to leave town right now. Thank you for caring for him." I paused just outside the barn doors. "Can you... Can you apologize to the girl in the inn for me? I was a bit harsh to her?"

He nodded.

"Thanks." I tossed him the last of my coins and kept Jericho moving.

We were trotting down the path when I heard Conri's voice at the edge of the forest, but I refused to look.

"Kassy!" Conri shouted. "Please, Kassy! Stay! I need to explain!"

I took a deep breath, urged Jericho on, and galloped away as fast as he could run.

I breathed a sigh of relief when I could no longer hear his voice, but only moments later Conri's voice was replaced with a mournful howl that nearly had me turning back. I tightened my jaw and continued running.

14
Wild Wolfe
Conri

*W*olfe went wild with despair. We ran hard until the moon had sunk and risen once again. Darkness settled on us as we searched for easy prey. Rabbits and squirrels fluttered about, but we craved more. Only blood could quell our pain.

The grunts and wheezes of a nearby buck grabbed our attention. We headed toward the sounds of his antlers scraping the hard bark of a nearby tree. Crouching in the underbrush, we stalked our prey. The deer stood tall and proud, yet he never stood a chance.

Blood boiled within our body. We wanted—no, we needed to kill something. The larger the better. This buck would satisfy us.

Our muscles tightened and burned as we crept out from the cover of the trees. The buck raised his head and snorted at us. His eyes tracked us as we paced before him, then the buck turned and ran.

Wolfe laughed in our head. The hunt was on. We sprinted off after the massive animal. Our breath grew ragged, burning our lungs as our wide paws pounded the ground. We ran faster and faster.

Gaining ground on the beast, we made one last push. He was within reach now. We lunged for the buck's hindquarters and clamped down hard. Our long canines cut through fur and into the thick muscle. Blood spurted from his leg, coating our mouth and draining down our chest. Warm and wet, we swallowed it down.

The buck collapsed to the ground before we released our hold. The taste of blood drove our hunger to new heights. Circling the dying beast, we watched his breathing fade away until it finally stopped. Our first kill in many moonrises sent a deep satisfaction throughout our body. Licking the blood from our muzzle, we dove in and began devouring our dinner.

With a full stomach, our mind seemed to clear, if only slightly. We knew the consequences of being a lone wolf for too long and had no desire to go down that road again.

We need to find Kelly and the others, I told Wolfe.

I know. I know, he barked back.

What about the Silver Silence? Won't they be tracking us the moment we leave? My sister was strong but still I worried for her safety.

There was only one of them. If we find the others and stick together he might leave us alone. Wolfe reasoned.

We breathed deep, slowing our heart rate. Our blood pumped through our veins faster and faster, causing our senses to go wild. We sniffed the cool night air, smelling nothing but wild forest. We jerked our head from side-to-side, breathing heavy.

I... I couldn't breathe. I needed to find help, but I couldn't see straight. I had loved Abrielle and her death nearly killed me. But Kassy.... If I couldn't be with her, I had nothing left. Forcing our body to stop in the middle of the woods, I took deep, gasping breaths.

Calm the fuck down, Conri, Wolfe scolded me. *We won't find anything if you panic. Let me find Kelly. You gonna let some pussy kill us now? You haven't even gotten your dick wet, and you're gonna let us die? Fuck you.*

Our legs shook, dropping us to the floor. Our heart thumped in our ears, drowning out any other sounds. The sky grew dark, and nothing surrounded us but the emptiness of the forest.

Wolfe

Thank the fucking gods he is out of my way.

Conri thinks too much. If he would have let me take her, we wouldn't be in this situation right now. But no, he wanted to let it be her choice, and now she was gone. I have half a mind to just go find her myself and fuck her wherever she is. But the look of horror on her face when she finally saw us froze me in place.

Damn it, Conri was right. She would hate us forever if I did that. I paced the forest floor, unsure of what to do next. Conri was the logical one. I was the one he called upon when something needed to die.

I let out a low howl and tucked my tail between my legs. Conri's pain was my pain. I grieved just as deeply for his loss as Conri did. I would have been content to lie here and die without her.

That was, until I smelled them.

There were only two of them, and they hadn't smelled me yet. I snarled with pure excitement. I crouched low as the unsuspecting wolves came into view.

Once they saw me, they glared wild-eyed at me, teeth bared, snarling their hatred. My claws gripped the earth beneath me as I flexed my muscled forelegs in anticipation. The buck had gone down easily. These two would bring a new challenge.

Both wolves pawed at the dirt as they circled me. I stood head and shoulders above these two peons. Still, the foolish wolves edged closer.

They ignored my growls, lunging for me. I dove under their attack, catching the gray one by the back paw. I bit down hard, spraying blood all over the ground.

The gray wolf yelped as I released him. With his tail firmly tucked between his legs, he limped backward. The other wolf was still on the offensive.

My hatred for Amarok grew. Forcing his way onto a seat of power he never earned was one thing, but sending these two pups to die on his behalf was pathetic. He knew they stood no chance of bringing me in, but he did it anyway. My vision grew hazy, and I saw red.

With a renewed hunger, I lunged for the black wolf's throat, clamping down hard. The wolf rolled, but I gripped my jaw tighter. Dust stirred around us, and the gray wolf's eyes trained on us, hesitating to join the fight. Finally, the black wolf stilled, and waited as his life energy poured out. His whine penetrated the surrounding air until finally he grew silent.

Turning to the other, I commanded him, *Go back and tell Amarok I'm coming for him.*

The wolf dragged his paws, reluctant to leave his friend's body.

Now! I snarled at him.

He lowered his head and backed away from me before turning to run off.

I licked the blood from my paws, craving more. Something changed within me. A deep need to see the wolves who had been hunting me for so long torn to shreds spread throughout my body. I didn't care that they were betas or that they were ordered to hunt me by their alphas.

The bloodlust grew, and I knew I was losing control. Those wolves might not have taken my mate from me, but they would pay for that pain as well.

A deeper howl ripped through me. I heard the distant whimpers of the wolf scout as I cried out in fury. Digging my paws into the earth, I launched forward. I'd hunt them all, just like they'd been hunting me.

15
Back to the Woods We Go

Scarlet

I have never been good with confrontation, so I retreated to my favorite hiding place: a tree. Jericho and I ran as far as we could get. I hunted for some meat once my head cleared. What I knew I couldn't eat I sold to a small village before riding off again.

After hours of traveling, a large shadow loomed over us. To my surprise, it appeared to be a barn. A small farm stretched out behind it. An older farmhand stepped out of the barn as Jericho and I approached. He was glad for the extra coin and stabled Jericho for me.

I found the largest tree I could, climbed up it, and tied myself to its branches. Using my pack as a makeshift pillow, I rested against the lumpy bag. Closing my eyes, I attempted to sleep, but my mind simply wouldn't shut off. My body still needed Conri, despite the fact that my head told me to flee. I needed his softness pressed up against my body to sleep. I needed his scent to breathe. The need to bury the past several days and move on burned deep within me, as did the need to see his face. I shut my eyes, desperate to see nothing, but only his smile came to my mind.

I wanted to kill something in hopes the blood would wash away the ache in my chest. I had promises to keep, and I couldn't let one man change my mind.

I have to avenge Rose and Nate's deaths.

I pulled the pack out from under me and unbuckled the straps. I dug around for the last of my jerky when my hand clasped around something hard. I pulled out the little figurine, and my finger stroked the wooden horse's back. My mind replayed the image of his rippling muscles as he threw that ball to win me this silly token. I smiled at the memory.

For such a big man, he shook as we neared the top of the Ferris wheel. He was terrified of heights, but he rode anyway... because I wanted him to. The tears fell before I knew to stop them. My heart didn't know if I loved him or hated him.

He had known what I was from day one, and yet he let me fall for him. He should have known how this would end. But yet... he hadn't killed me.

No, I should have never gotten involved. I should have known better. I considered all his elusive answers. He had told me so many half-truths. What kind of human gets shot by his own people? And he had nothing with him but a small pack that day I found him in the forest. He had no weapons and no tools. For gods sake the man couldn't even shoot. He had never even told me which village he was from or what he did for money. Why hadn't I asked more questions? Why hadn't I demanded more answers?

I shoved the little toy in my pack and tied it back up. I loosened the ropes from around my middle and began my climb down the tree. I hadn't seen any movement here since I arrived this morning. It was time to move on. Once my feet hit solid ground, I pulled the ropes from the branch above and packed them up too.

I knocked a bolt into my crossbow before walking on. Holding the bow tight to my shoulder, I walked as silently as I could. My eyes scanned the trees for movement. I walked half the night before I allowed myself to relax, if only slightly.

I lowered my bow as I walked a little taller. I couldn't find anything to hunt here. I thought about heading home, but that would mean admitting defeat. The Huntsmen would laugh me out of town. I had to bring home at least one pelt or else I'd never be able to show my face again.

Besides, Jericho and I had been traveling for days. Home was far behind us.

Just as I thought of the hopelessness of my situation, I saw a flash of white in my periphery. I turned, quickly raising my bow, but it was gone. I scanned the area, looking for whatever was stalking me. A noise to my right sent me spinning around again.

I fired my bolt just as the blur vanished again.

Damn. This wolf is fast.

I nocked another, walking toward where my last one fell. I circled, searching for any sign of the wolf, and when I saw nothing, I cursed under my breath. After another moment, I knelt down to retrieve the arrow from the forest floor. I heard the growl before the breath puffed over the back of my neck.

I dropped my bow and turned around so fast, it made my head spin. The snarling face towered over me, sending me scurrying backward in the mud, further away from my bow that was just out of reach.

My heart jumped in my throat. I opened my eyes wide and clasped my hand around the hilt of my knife at my side. It was small and mostly useless when it came to killing a wolf, but it was all I had.

The wolf's growl turned to a whimper, and I stared through wide eyes. The white beast was so small it had to be a female. I'd heard they were more wild than the males yet this wolf had laid her body to the ground at my feet. She continued to whine as I scrambled back away from her and toward my crossbow. My hand gripped the butt of the weapon as I pulled myself to my feet.

The cowering wolf's eyes were fixed on me, prepared to die, as I stood over her with my crosshairs on her chest.My hands shook as I watched her. She made no move to run or attack. She just sat there, staring at me with her blue eyes.

"What the hell?" I whispered into the darkness.

Werewolves were wild, but they were seldom unpredictable. I had just been under her fangs, but she had clearly submitted to me. Willingly. In that moment, I was not dominant to her, yet she had given me control.

"What are you?" I asked her. I lowered my bow and removed the bolt. Kneeling, I laid the bow on the ground beside me. Our eyes locked.

An invisible force moved my hand out toward this wolf. Still, she made no movement. I gently grazed the fur between her ears. Fear melted away at the warmth of her fur. She made a noise that made me think of a human sigh and I let myself scratch her a little deeper.

As my palm connected with her fur, an image flew into my mind of the wolf Conri had turned into, and he wasn't alone. Another, smaller white wolf nuzzled close to him. A peace like no other filled me.

I pulled my hand away, grabbed my crossbow, and jumped onto my feet in an instant.

"What was that?" I breathed. The wolf just watched me. I aimed my bow straight at the wolf's face. Neither of us moved. I should have taken the shot, but I ran instead. I dragged my crossbow with me, slinging my pack over my shoulders as I ran. My feet didn't stop moving until I got back to the barn I had left Jericho in.

The farmhand looked at me with concern when I stumbled into the barn, gasping for air.

"You okay, Miss?" he asked me.

"I…I…I'm fine, thank you." I straightened, brushing the dried mud from my pants. "I need my horse. What do I owe you?" My eyes scanned the woods behind the barn. Squirrels skittered around the forest floor as birds chattered from the trees. I found no sign of the wolf.

"Honestly, Miss, we haven't even fed him yet. He's been out in the pasture since you left him. He even refused to come in or even eat treats. It's been no trouble." The man walked over to the wall, pulling his reins off, and handing them to me. "He's all yours. Do you want a saddle? I have an extra one I'd sell you cheap."

I only considered the man's offer for a moment. I rubbed at my sore ass and winced at the thought of riding bareback again. "Sure, that's fine. Thank you."

"What happened to yours?" he asked as he pulled a saddle from the stand and walked toward the paddock.

"I...I left the last town in a hurry, and I didn't have time to saddle him."

"Seems like a lot of money to waste," he scoffed.

Fear had consumed me when I ran from Conri. The pain in his voice as he shifted from human to wolf tore through me. The images of Rose and Nate's bodies flashed in my mind, knowing that Conri was capable of such destruction. But another kind of fear filled me now: never again having those lips brush against mine or his body pressed against me. I pushed the thoughts aside as I refocused on the problems at hand.

"I couldn't help it. It had to be done."

"Your money, I guess." The older gentleman strode over to Jericho. He handed me a bucket full of water, and I quickly washed the dirt from the horse's body. When I was done, the kind farmhand handed me a brush before I finally saddled him.

I gave the farmhand some of the last coins from my pouch and mounted my horse. I urged Jericho once more toward the forest. I didn't know where I was headed. I just needed to get as far from these wolves as I could.

I knew where we were headed before the woods thinned. I pressed down the memories of the last time I had run to Whitegulf. Sunlight streamed down on us, and the cool air of the forest disappeared. I stuck to the larger roads, hoping to get as far from the woods as I could.

Leaving the woods behind was like leaving a part of myself. My body shook as reality settled over me. The wolves terrified me but I, at least, knew what to expect of them… or at least I had. But humans were deceptively kind. They'd seem like they cared only to stab you in the back. At least with the wolves, I knew what they wanted. All except for Conri. I resisted the urge to turn back toward the trees once more. I wasn't just leaving the woods behind, I was leaving a part of myself. I was losing everything I was.

My chest tightened, and my breathing slowed. An ache I couldn't describe seemed to fill me. Jericho walked down the dusty road as I silently cried.

16
Killer Wolf
Wolfe

*C*onri was gone, and only I remained. Tattered and broken as I was, I knew I had to keep myself sane if we were to survive this. Few did though. It was rare but the last time a true mate rejected the other, the wolf threw himself off a cliff. *He's weak but I'm not.* I had to gain control, but…

Blood. Death. Pain. That was all I could see; all I wanted to show the world.

I wanted to ignore the stabbing pain in my chest. I always thought Conri was the weak one, but now I was just as weak. My guts twisted inside of me. Uncertainty filled me, and in all the moons I had walked this ground, I had never experienced such loss. The world was spinning a little too fast, and I no longer cared if it flung me right off the surface, out into space. Without her, nothing else mattered.

I stuck my muzzle into the dirt, breathing in the dozens of different scents buried beneath my paws. A low whine escaped me. I could still smell her.

I was pounding my paws against the dirt before I had given it a second thought. I followed her scent, blocking out all others. There was only her. The faint lavender I had grown to love, now mixed with salt, was growing stronger and stronger. The sounds of the town grew closer. I didn't even care that I was still in my wolf form. I'd find her.

Something massive collided with my side, sending me crashing through the trees. Pain rippled down my spine as my back slammed into the hard bark. Half-a-dozen wolves surrounded me. I didn't care. I wanted to get to my mate.

Pushing past one, I tried to pick up her trail again. The stench of the wild beasts overwhelmed her scent. Fangs sank into my tail, dragging me back inside the circle of enemy wolves. I snarled back at them. Every hair along my neck stood on end. I was so blinded by my rage I couldn't tell which one lunged first. I only knew he went down easy.

His blood coated my fur. I flung his body to the side with ease. My grin widened as I picked up the first scent of fear among my attackers.

I do hope he wasn't one of your best. His blood tastes a little sour. I licked my jowls.

You bastard. One of them snarled.

Conri wasn't the Sage for his pretty face, I told them. *He knew I'd happily destroy all those that failed us. It has been so long since I have hunted. I will enjoy this.* Fire burned within me, begging to be let loose on these fools. I growled low.

They backed up a step.

C-Conri? The voice cracked as it asked for the more merciful human.

I am Wolfe. Everything about Conri is gone, and only the monster remains. I have longed to kill freely again, and here I am with such willing prey.

They froze.

I racked up my death count. I lunged for the closest one, clenching his front paw in my teeth. My jaws snapped shut, snapping his bones in two. I quickly silenced his whimper when my fangs tore through his throat.

Who's next? I questioned the group. A mix of growls and yips came from the remaining wolves.

Another charged me from behind, sinking his teeth into my hindquarters. I flung my hips around, pinning him into a tree. He whined as he tried to stand. The others parted as I walked toward him. I stood over his broken form.

Never be so low that you sneak up on your enemy. If you are going to fight, have the guts to face me.

The wolf slowly got to his feet, nipping at me. With a swift movement, I snapped his neck. His limp body fell to the forest floor.

The distant sounds of cheers pulled my focus toward the town just long enough for two more wolves to attack.

One clamped down on my back paw while another bit down on my flank. I howled in pain. The clamor from the townsfolk in the distance quieted.

I snarled as I twisted my body around, snapping at the one on my leg. He released me and backed away. I dropped to the ground, rolling onto my back, and throwing the other off me.

I was growing tired of this game.

I peered around in the darkness. There were only three left. The ground was soft beneath me as I launched my body forward. I sank my fangs into his throat, ripping it to shreds, spraying blood everywhere. Hot crimson liquid coated my face. I licked my jaws as his body fell to the forest floor.

My eyes met the fearful gazes of the last two. *Do you want to continue this contest?* I asked them. One lowered his gaze. The other growled and lunged.

He fell to the ground in a heap before he took another step. Blood and muck from the forest floor caked my body.

A deep growl rumbled within me as I stared at the last remaining wolf.

I just tore through five of you within mere moments. Do you want to become the sixth?

He lowered his body to the ground in submission.

C-Conri...Wolfe...I'm sorry. Forgive my weakness. I...I was afraid of Amarok. I wish to be loyal to only you, but....

But what? Do you think I want a coward like you? You are either loyal to me or to Amarok. You cannot change sides when one is losing. You go back to your master and tell him of your cowardice. Tell him that I let you live only to deliver a message. I licked the blood from my paws like the wolf before me was boring.

Y-yes, Sage? What message do you want me to deliver to Amarok? The wolf trembled from nose to tail as he spoke.

Tell him I will come home and face his Trials. Tell him, when I defeat his Trials, it will be his turn to face mine. I turned my attention back to the shaking wolf. *And anyone who stands at his side will join him in his death.*

I nipped at the wolf, tearing the tip of his ear off in one bite. He yelped and rolled over the moment I released him.

Now go deliver the message, I barked.

The wolf slowly backed out of my reach before he turned and ran. A distant, mournful howl echoed in my head. I looked around at the mess I had created and smiled.

After the ruckus I had caused, I doubted anyone but scavengers would find the bodies. It was fitting that the trash that attacked me would be carried off with the rats.

I sought out her scent again. But all I could smell was blood and rot. A wave of panic climbed up my throat. I needed to see her one last time before I headed toward my death. Even if she wouldn't have me, I still needed to gaze upon her face.

You pathetic human. Your emotions are clouding my thoughts, I barked at myself.

I am Wolfe. Not some weak human to be bound to another. The lie burned to my core. I needed my Kassy. I had to shake the weakness and hopelessness, but no matter how much I wanted to ignore it, the image of Kassy's smile kept flashing in my mind.

I needed to get a hold of myself if I were to survive the Trials.

I was the one that had claimed her. The bond wasn't completed yet, but she was mine. I needed her as much as Conri had, but that was a weakness I needed to squash. She had chosen her path and, as far as I was concerned, she was dead. But even the thought of her possible death brought bile to my throat.

The sooner I accepted that she was dead to us, the stronger I would be.

Just as I was about to walk away, I caught a tiny whiff of her. The sweet aroma of lavender now lacked the anxious, salty scent. She was far off, but she was there on the wind. All thoughts of leaving fled my mind as I focused on her. She was all I wanted. All I needed.

Death was waiting for me, and I would greet it like an old friend, but I had to say goodbye to my mate first.

I sniffed the air as I entered the dense trees. She had come this way a while ago. My nose followed the scent until it grew stronger. I ran deeper into the forest, following her.

This time, I kept my senses awake. My ears twitched at the sounds of an owl hooting high above, but I kept moving forward. Faster and faster, I ran toward my love. I think I would have allowed her to kill me just to be near her.

I had fallen into bloodlust once before, and I was flirting with the edge of sanity. To follow a woman that could kill you as easily as she breathes was the very definition of insanity.

I had fought all my life. I had fought to be Sage. I had fought to stay alive. Now I would willingly walk into her embrace, even if it meant she would slaughter me without a second thought.

My obsession grew the faster I ran.

My paws dug into the earth as I slid to a stop. Her trail had run cold. I sniffed the dirt, digging my muzzle deeper, desperate for just a hint of her. Nothing. I paced around, trying to find her again, but still I smelled nothing. A deep howl tore through me. I sat on my haunches and howled until dawn.

17
Brothels, Bar Fights, & Bars
Scarlet

$\mathcal{T}$he full moon would rise soon, and I couldn't trust myself to be out in the forest with the wolves running amok. Not now. My heart ached at the loss. I wanted Conri. I wanted to hunt. But I couldn't have either. Hunting was all I knew and now I had nothing. Wanting nothing more than to drown my sorrows, I led Jericho ever closer to town.

The people of Whitegulf didn't care that I was a female Hunter. My gold was as shiny as everyone else's. I needed a release, one I couldn't find back home. I also needed a good, stiff drink.

I left Jericho hitched outside of the brothel, Siren's Call, before walking inside. No one stopped to stare at me as I walked up to the bar in my red cloak. The reek of men that desperately needed a shower overwhelmed me. They sat at the tables that surrounded the bar, ignoring me.

The few male prostitutes who walked the floor averted their eyes when I tried to catch their attention. I scoffed as I stepped up to the bar.

"What can I do for you?" the shapely bartender asked me. She wore a black corset with thin lace fabric under it showing the outline of her breasts. Her skimpy skirt showed off her back side and thigh-high boots made her six inches taller. Her dirty-blonde hair fell down around her heart-shaped face. Her green eyes stared at me as I gaped back at her.

"You want something to drink, hun?" she asked again.

I gulped hard. "Yeah…whiskey." I tossed a few coins down. "And leave the bottle, please." I tried to keep the desperation out of my voice.

"Sure thing." She reached behind her, pulling a bottle from the shelf. I grabbed the nearly full bottle before she could reach for a glass and guzzled the spicy liquid down like it was water. Wiping the liquid from my lips, I slammed the now half-empty bottle down on the bar.

"That bad, eh?" She raised her eyebrow at me.

"Yeah…" was all I could say.

"What happened?"

I took another swig. My head was already spinning. I tried to ignore her stare, but those eyes were mesmerizing.

"Come on, sweetie. You can tell me."

I wiped a tear from my eye. "He's a…" I couldn't say the words out loud.

Her hand grazed over my skin sending a shiver down my spine. "No judgment here, hun."

My chest burned with the need to tell someone, anyone. I took another swig from the whiskey. "He's a fucking wolf!" I half-shouted at the woman. I teetered on the rickety barstool, nearly losing my balance.

"And I take it from the bow and the red cape that you're Scarlet?" she grinned.

"Yeah. See the dilemma?"

"Oh, I do." Her voice was velvety. "Why bother with men, anyway? They are so troublesome."

"I thought I…. I thought I could…." I couldn't bring myself to utter the painful words and allowed the whiskey to burn the emotions away.

"You thought you loved him?" She grinned slightly. "Wolves aren't all bad. Just rougher than most men."

My jaw dropped. Had this barmaid been with a werewolf? I sat staring at the woman as her hands traveled the length of her as if in remembrance of someone's touch. I opened my mouth to speak, but she spoke first.

"So why come here?" she asked.

I shook my head, trying to focus on her question. My brain reached for speech.

"Why come here?" she asked again more forcefully, and speech finally returned to me.

"I…I thought if I paid someone, they could erase him from my memory, if for just a moment."

She slid out from behind the bar and grazed my shoulder with her soft hand. I turned to face her, leaning against the back of the seat. Her slender fingers traced my jawline, then up to my lips. My knees shook with her touch. She brushed the tears away with her soft lips and my brain turned to mush, destroying all thoughts of werewolves.

She stepped closer to me, parting my knees and enveloping me in her rose scent. I set the bottle down, nearly spilling it.

"I... I..." I couldn't stop staring at the beautiful woman before me. Her skin was silky smooth, and her smile lit up the room. I longed for her long hair to slip between my fingers but couldn't force myself to reach out.

"Oh, you've never?" she pulled back slightly.

"No.... Not with a.... But...." I wrapped my hands around her waist, resting them just above her rather voluptuous backside. I pulled her closer. "I think I could if you help me."

She whispered in my ear, "I'll be gentle." Her lips were soft against mine.

My mouth moved with hers, parting slightly. Her tongue brushed against my lips. All sounds around us vanished, leaving only the sound of the thrumming of my heart as it echoed in my ears. I let my fingers gather and bunch up the meager fabric of her skirt until I slid my hand under the hem. She pulled my leg up and around her waist.

Stop. His voice echoed in my ears. I shut my eyes and imagined it was his ass I was grabbing, not some barmaid's.

Her lips moved from mine to my neck and I let my mind think his scratchy beard tickled my skin.

"You wanna go upstairs?" she breathed. Her hands traveled under my shirt, cupping my breast. I gave in to the temptation and rocked my hips to hers. She needed me as much as I needed her.

"Yeah," I finally breathed back. "But aren't you still working?"

"I'm just about done with my shift anyway. Let's go have some fun." A wicked smile spread across her face.

Just as I stood, her eyes bulged for a second before a man behind her flung her roughly to the side. The giant of a man stood, looming in front of me, glaring daggers at me.

"What the fuck you think you're doing?" He glared at me like I should bother to answer him.

My head was swimming, so I only shrugged.

"Why don't you go fuck one of the guys? Better yet, go fuck yourself! You're the only one that'll have a bitch like you! We don't need your kind 'round here." He raised his hand and struck me across the face before I could blink.

I fell to the hard floor with a thud. My buzz fled from my body as quickly as it had come. My fingers found the hilt of the knife in my boot. My face stung, but the heat that boiled within me burned away any fear. I took a few calming breaths before I faced the man. His greasy locks fell down his back and over his shoulders, mixing with his beard. He smelled like cheap ale and vomit.

I hid the knife behind my back as I stood. My lips turned upward in what I hoped to be an innocent smile. "I don't understand. What's the problem?" I asked.

"Bridget ain't for the likes of you," he shouted back.

"Oh, and she's for you then?" I looked at the woman who now cowered in the corner. "She doesn't look like she's that interested."

"Watch it, or I'll beat your ass like the bitch you are."

I bowed low. "Yes, Sire. Please, m'lord, I'd love another." I made my voice as pleasing as I could.

"That's it! Why don't I take you upstairs and show you your place?"

"Please, Sire. Take me and fill me." I grinned wider. "If you can…." I licked my lips imagining what his blood would taste like on my tongue. Images of every man that ever thought they could take what they wanted filled me. Starting with my first kill all those winters ago at camp. My hands shook that day but tonight, my hands were steady. I regretted little of that death, but this man… He'd pay for the sins of men, and I'd smile with each hit.

Just as he lunged for me, I sidestepped, sending him crashing into the barstool behind me. I didn't suppress the laughter that escaped me now.

His roar got the attention of everyone in the bar. Out of the corner of my eye, I saw Bridget grab a cloak and dart out the front door. I turned back to look at my opponent.

My vision was clearing as I watched him straighten. He stood nearly as tall as Conri and twice as wide, but he was fat and slow. I may never get the chance to take my rage out on Conri but I'd willingly give it to this filth.

I smiled at him, waiting for him to make his next move. He shook his head and glared at me.

"You fucking come here!" He lunged, but I stepped to the side. He fell forward, and I brought my knee to his nose.

I pulled the knife from behind my back. "No, sweetie. Why don't you come here? I'd love to get closer to you." I leaned over him as the man wailed in pain.

He crawled on his knees away from me. Pushing against the edge of the bar, he stepped back. Blood covered his hands as he held them to his broken nose. After a second, he raised his fists again. "You are a fucking crazy bitch."

"There are still plenty more bones to be broken or things to be cut off." I let my eyes drift down his dirty pants. The drunkard's eyes grew wide as he finally understood.

Neither of us moved for a long moment.

The front door shattered the silence as it slammed open. Five heavily armed men strode inside. These were no drunkards hoping to pay for companionship. Their cloaks were mostly clean, and their swords were certainly sharpened. Three of the men had drawn longswords, and two archers had arrows nocked and bows drawn. They spread throughout the room as other patrons hurried out of their way. In seconds, they had surrounded both me and my attacker.

The sound of a thud echoed behind me, but I didn't bother to look. I knew it was the drunkard falling to his fat ass again.

I laid my knife on the floor and raised my arms. "I was only defending myself. He attacked me first." I spoke calmly, internally assessing the situation. No way would I get out of here alive if these men decided I was a threat.

"We know. Bridget told us everything. Still, a night in a cell might do you both some good." The old man in the middle spoke. His graying mustache covered his lips and his wide-brim hat covered his eyes.

I turned to glare at him. His shaggy salt and pepper hair hung loosely around his brow. His thin lips pursed, nearly disappearing beneath his thick mustache. His ice-blue eyes looked from me to the man behind me.

"Don't you worry, Miss. We will keep you far away from each other," he reassured me.

"Fine. Now, will you lower your weapons? I'm unarmed." None of the men loosened their grips on their swords, and the two archers didn't bother to lower their bows. Their focus clearly wasn't on the disgusting man swaying behind me. Their weapons were for me.

"Well, the thing is, Miss Scarlet, we all know you're a Huntsman, and yer clearly a bit tanked. We'd feel safer if you just follow us." His cool eyes never left mine.

I rolled my eyes, but I complied. The room was still spinning a bit, and something inside of me still urged me to beat the foul man behind me until he could no longer move.

Perhaps they had a point. Besides, it had been far too long since I actually slept on a bed.

I kept my hands raised as I walked past them. Two men passed behind me. Their eyes were wary as they sheathed their swords. With a great grunt, they lifted my attacker to his feet.

The smell of the man overcame me again, causing my stomach to turn. I watched as both of his guards leaned away from the smell.

"Perhaps you could douse him in one of the horse troughs before bringing him along," I said, waving my hand in front of my nose. Two men fought back their laughter.

"She has a point," I heard the younger one on the left whisper.

The sheriff led the way back through the brothel. Bridget stood at the door, holding it open for me. She stopped me when I neared. Her fingers brushed the place where the man's hand had struck me.

"I'm sorry," she whispered.

"It's okay." I nuzzled my face into her hand.

She leaned in, briefly brushing her lips against mine. "Not just for this man, but for your wolf. If you really love him, can he be forgiven?"

She stepped back before I could respond. Two guards appeared at my side. One shoved me roughly, urging me on.

"You should really reconsider whether you want to do that." I stopped to eye the guard who had shoved me. "The last man who did it doesn't look so good right now."

Behind us, the drunkard had begun to heave his dinner and his drink into the street. Blood still poured from his nose.

The guard didn't reply, but he also didn't shove me again. We walked down the street until we came to the local jailhouse. The old man stepped inside first, opening the cell door. I walked into the room and sat on the small cot against the back wall. The sheriff closed the cell door before the other men lowered their weapons.

"Sorry 'bout this, Miss Scarlet, but it'll be safer for all of us this way," he said apologetically.

"'S'okay. I really do understand. Just make sure my horse and things are safe, please?" I said, laying back on the cot.

He nodded, and one of the guards left to follow the silent order.

The two men carrying the drunkard walked through the door when the sheriff stopped them with a hand in the air. "Do not bring him back in here until he smells less like a latrine and has seen the healer." The sheriff spoke.

I laughed to myself as I pulled the thin cotton blanket up to my shoulders.

"My wife will bring us some dinner." I wasn't sure if the sheriff was talking to me or the guards as he sat in his chair, placing his feet on the desk. "Settle in boys. It'll be a late night."

18
Over the River
Scarlet

The thin padding on the cot did little to aid my need for rest. The hay poked through the thin fabric and made my eyes water while the whiskey still buzzed in my head. Not even my thick red cape could keep me from shivering. I lay there all night, watching the world spin. The nausea in my stomach made falling into a deep slumber impossible.

No matter how much I tried to think about home or Nate or Rose or anything else to keep my mind off him, all I saw was Conri's face dropping to the forest floor in agony. He was so terrified that night, and I hadn't put everything together yet. He was screaming for it to all stop and only now did I finally understand that he was yelling at his wolf.

How had I not seen that he was a wolf? I had been so blinded by... by what? Some invisible force pulling us together? I had refused to see all the warnings that were now so clear. I had been trained to believe a wolf could no longer be human, and I cursed the commanding officers for not knowing the truth.

Maybe I could go back and be a better trainer to the new recruits. But how could I. I was too blinded by how tight his ass was and how his giant size made that room look like a fucking doll house to notice his impossible hearing and fast healing.

He'd looked at me with pride after fighting those trainees, which had my heart fluttering. Tears stung my eyes as I remembered back to the way his arms held me when I was afraid to sleep.

The memories ended with Bridget, and the man I'd fought in the bar, and guilt churned my stomach at what I had nearly done and what Conri would say if he knew I had almost slept with someone that wasn't him. I punched the bed and wiped the tears from my eyes.

Why do I care about what he thinks?

As much as I fought it, I kept coming back to the strange desire to do him no harm, but I had hurt him. The sound of his howls as I ran away still haunted me, and they tore through me like that arrow had torn through his shoulder. I lay in that jail and wept silently until dawn arrived.

The clinking of keys and footsteps nearing the cell reminded me I was not alone. I stifled the tears and sat up just as the old sheriff approached the doors. I had to shield my eyes from the morning sun peeking through the doorway as I rearranged myself on the cot.

"How ya feeling?" His tone was gentle. I was positive I wasn't the first nor the last drunken idiot to sleep one off in his cell.

Rubbing at my stomach, I sat up. "Eh. I've had better days." The aroma of bacon and eggs filled the room. As my eyes adjusted to the morning light, I noticed a tray with two plates in his hands.

"You up for some breakfast? Wife made it special for you," he grinned. "She heard *the* Scarlet was in my jail cell."

I groaned. I'd never get away from that name. But I nodded my head anyway. He unlocked the cell door and motioned for me to follow him. We sat at an empty desk in the small room. I hesitated before taking the first bite of food. The whiskey still burned in my stomach.

"So, you wanna talk 'bout what happened last night?" the old sheriff asked.

"Not really." I swallowed my eggs.

"Seems to me you need to talk to someone. I've heard just 'bout everything."

I rolled my eyes. "Not this."

"Maybe not, but you won't hear a judgmental tone outta me." His gentle prodding reminded me of my father before Rose's death. The sheriff's blue eyes held my gaze as he ate his food. I got the distinct impression he would not let me leave without saying something.

I gulped the warm tea he offered me before I started. "Well, you already know I'm a Huntsman."

"Aye. I figured that much out pretty quickly. I've heard the rumors of the legendary Scarlet and judging by the broken nose on your friend last night, they're all probably true."

"I was out hunting when this man came blundering through the forest. He was bleeding and panicking. I helped him." I tried to push the tears back. I don't know why, but I knew I couldn't tell this old man the truth about what I had seen Conri turn into. I knew it sounded crazy.

"You fell in love?"

I cocked my head, surprised that he had guessed so quickly.

"Someone only drinks like that when they're heartbroken." The sheriff shrugged as he took another long swig of his tea.

I nodded. "But he's…" I couldn't say the words.

His eyes softened. He polished off his plate in silence before he spoke again. "Sounds like you're in a pickle, for sure."

"But he's a—"

"Wolf?" He cocked an eyebrow.

"You know… what he is?" I stammered.

"Whitegulf is a bit of a rough town Miss. We're so far off the beaten path that most Huntsmen don't bother paying us a visit. We see all sorts here, and your man isn't the first wolf to pass through town."

"Wait? What?"

"It's true, Miss. We've known about the shifters for a while now. For the most part they don't pay us no mind, so we leave them be. In fact, this is the most excitement we've had in our town in a while." He took a long sip from the coffee cup before he continued. "We've tried to tell the rest of Breton that the wolves can change and we can live in peace but we're just a bunch of criminals to most of the world." He stared at me for a long moment. "So, what are you going to do about your problem?" he asked.

I stared off into nothing for a long time. Everything I thought I knew was a lie and others knew the truth. I couldn't process what I'd just been told. I tried to focus on one problem at a time, though. I thought of all the reasons I came to Whitegulf in the first place and what I could do instead.

"Honestly, I don't know. I don't know what I'm going to do. The reason I came here in the first place is I can't hunt. I tried...but I missed. And I never miss. If I can't hunt, I can't go back home. I have nothing."

And I refused to go to the Isles with every other former Huntsman.

I was so exhausted physically and emotionally that I could no longer hold the tears back and although this man was a total stranger, he seemed like someone who would keep my words safe.

"You got anywhere else to go? Least 'till you straighten yourself out?"

I took another sip from my mug. The rich aroma brought me back to my Saba's kitchen, watching him cook. The aroma of coffee and whispered conversations waking me every morning and him teaching which foods in the forest were edible. I smiled at the memories. "Maybe...if he'll have me. Been a while since I've seen him."

"He family?" I nodded. "Then he'll always have your back." A comforting hand came to rest on my shoulder. I hadn't even realized the man had left his chair. "I had my boys gather your things for ya, and your horse is out front. I suggest ya take off 'fore the rest of the town wakes up."

I placed my mug on the desk and stood. He offered me a hand that I gratefully shook. "Thanks."

"My pleasure, ma'am. One more thing. I hate to be the bastard, but..."

"Don't worry. I won't be back. I don't think I could stand the looks." He nodded his thanks and walked me to the door. I wrapped my cloak tighter and raised the hood over my head. The brisk morning air swept around me.

I mounted Jericho and headed out of town. Even though I hated towns, this one could possibly be a home for me eventually and I'd miss the friends I had made within. I rode past The Siren's Call, my eyes finding Bridget's sad, smiling face as she stood on the porch, and I nodded my silent thanks. No matter what happened, I'd always remember her kindness.

19
And through the Woods

Scarlet

The sun lit up the old cabin that stood in the valley in the middle of the only clearing for hundreds of clicks. I guided my horse over the narrow bridge that spanned the small creek in front of his house. I hadn't been here in many winters, but the sunlight hitting the small garden was heaven to my sad eyes. Memories of eating tomatoes straight off the vine came flooding back to me. I was so close, I could taste the juices flowing down my chin, and hear the snapping of peas as I sat on the porch with my Saba preparing the evening meal.

Tying Jericho to the hitching post, I strode in through the front door without knocking.

The fire in the hearth spread warmth throughout the tiny house, and the pine wood burning wrapped me in an aroma that reminded me of when I was a child. I used to sit in the rocker with Saba and listen to his tales until the embers were all but extinguished.

"Hiya, kiddo. Been a minute since you visited me here," Saba said without turning from the fire. I smiled. "I figured I'd be seeing you soon."

For the first time in my life, I realized how odd it was that he always knew what to expect. Up until now, it had been part of his special Saba powers that just made him who he is, but with everything that had happened in the last few weeks, it took me aback.

He waddled over to me, showing no concern at my hesitation and took my pack and hung my cloak on the rack beside the door. His short, stout stature and his bulbous nose overshadowed his thin lips always made me smile. He rested my pack behind the door and wrapped me in a hug. I still couldn't wrap my arms around his round frame.

He guided me over to the hearth, sitting me down in our old rocker and stared at me with those eyes that always knew when I needed to talk. I pulled my boots off, tossing them by the fire.

"What brings you to my neck of the woods during huntin' season?" My grandfather was always so observant and knew me so well. I just wasn't sure I could talk about it yet. Not even to him.

"I just missed ya, is all." I averted my eyes.

"All righty, then…" He dragged out the words. "You keep your secrets. There's stew in the pot." He pointed to the cast-iron hanging over the fire.

"Not hungry at the moment." I set my feet on the edge of the chair and wrapped my arms around my knees.

"Oh, pish. Eat some bread at least." He handed me a slice of sourdough. "Bread can cure any weary heart, my dear."

I bit into the warm bread, and I couldn't help but agree just a little.

"Maybe not every weary heart," I whispered to myself.

"You came to me, sweetheart." His blue eyes stared through me waiting for an answer.

"I know, Saba. Just… not tonight, eh? It's been a long season already." I slumped back into the chair and curled my knees up to my chest. Everything that had happened since the morning I left my village weighed on my mind once more. Tears burned in my eyes as I pushed the memories away.

Saba stood and walked over to me again. His eyes were solemn as he leaned down and kissed the crown of my head.

"Alright, kiddo. I'll get you some blankets."

I laid down on the spare cot in the corner, looking up at the hand-hewn wooden beams. Saba had built this cabin himself from the trees off his land. He had to have been near sixty when he came out here yet he managed to build this home.

I pushed the thoughts from my head and fell into a deep sleep before Saba had even come back to lay the blankets over me.

The moment I fell asleep, I was running for my life and gasping for air. The trees flew past me in a blur. I heard the snapping of branches from my pursuers close on my heels. I urged my feet to run faster. I had discarded my crossbow a while back because it was far too heavy. My hands gripped the hilts of my knives instead.

My chest burned as my lungs strained to keep pace with my feet. Tears streamed down my cheeks, and my vision blurred. I couldn't outrun them much longer. I would have to turn and fight. I wasn't sure what good it would do me, but I was a Huntsman, and I would never go down that easily.

I ran until my legs ached and I feared my heart would stop its furious beating in my chest.

It was now or never. I slowed my pace and found a wide tree to take shelter behind. I leaned against the bark, steadying my breathing.

The snorts of their muzzles on the ground stopped my breathing all together. They were right behind me.

"Little Red?" One of them called.

"Where are you?" They were taunting me.

"Come out, come out wherever you are," I heard the first laugh.

I gulped hard before I slid out from behind my hiding spot to face them. Ice burned through my veins, freezing me in place at the faces staring back at me. My pursuers were not the werewolves I thought had been hunting me, but those of my family.

The name that had once filled me with joy now ran through me like nails. My father had called me Little Red, a childhood nickname long before I earned the name Scarlet. My mother stood beside him, smiling like she was eager to see my death. My Saba stood beside his son who had long ago disowned him. I could only assume the woman beside my Saba was my grandmother. They all held makeshift weapons and smiled at me as if this were an ordinary day.

Another voice snuck up behind me, startling me. His massive arms wrapped around my middle, pulling me against his chest as he spoke. "Oh my, Scarlet. How I have missed you. Can you tell just how much?" Conri pressed his hard cock into the small of my back. His rough hands pushed my head to one side, yanking the strands of my hair. He raked his teeth against my neck. "I want you more than you can imagine." His protruding fangs clamped down on my sensitive flesh, causing blood to stream down my throat.

"No!" I screamed, trying to wriggle free, but his grip tightened.

"Tut-tut-tut. Is that anyway to treat your mate?" His tongue licked my neck. I screamed as his fangs punctured deeper into my flesh.

My cries shattered the silence of the night around me. My hands reached for the spot where Conri's fangs had just been. I sighed when I found nothing but my damp sweat. Sitting up, I looked around the unfamiliar room. When I spotted the old rocking chair, I sighed, knowing I was safe. The musty scent of my Saba's cabin filled me, bringing me a sense of comfort.

The dying embers of the fire lit up the room enough to see the silhouette of my Saba as he stepped into the small space, holding a steaming cup of tea. He handed it to me before pulling the old rocker along with him and stopping just in front of my cot. He leaned back against the old slats with a comfortable sigh.

"Care to tell me why you were just screaming like you were being torn to shreds?"

"I…. It was a nightmare." I took a long swig. The hot tea burned my throat, but I didn't care. The sensation only pulled me further away from my nightmare.

"I think it was more than just a nightmare." He raised a brow at me.

"I was being chased…I thought by werewolves, but it was…it was you. You, dad, mom…" I trailed off, not able to finish my thoughts. I stared down at the swirling amber liquid trying to clear the memories from my mind.

"Well, you're safe. Nothing to worry about now."

I sat back on the cot and tried to push the images out of my mind.

"Saba?"

"Yes, kiddo?"

"My life's gone a little crazy. I'm not sure what I'm gonna do. Can I stay here for a bit?" I asked him sheepishly.

He stood, taking my now empty mug from my hands. "Sure thing, but you know staying here ain't free? You gotta help me out 'round here. You hear me?"

"Yes, Saba," I agreed as I settled back under the covers.

20

Enlisting Help
Wolfe

Rage boiled within me. My vision blurred, and I saw red for the second time. The copper and rot stench of their blood that clung to my fur burned my nose. I had discarded their lifeless forms like the trash they were and walked around the forest, just daring the others to come.

My muscles burned for another fight. I was never good at sitting still and I longed for the familiar thrill of the hunt to drown out the aching in my heart. Her image came to me again as I continued pacing. She lay beneath me with that perfect body just begging to be taken. But Conri had pussed out and ran. What would have been the point in my trying to stop him? He never listened to me anyway, so I let him run and hide like he always has. He had ruined everything. Now we were out here, alone in the wild, waiting to be attacked again.

The first one stalked into my little clearing like I wasn't there. His snarls made me laugh. I stood over him like a man stood over an ant. I could squish him in an instant. I howled my amusement at the lone wolf.

My head swiveled as I watched the others slowly surround me, not as many as the last time, but these were stronger. *Amarok's a coward.* He'd never be able to defeat me in a fair fight so he was working his way up his ranks to get to me. It was sheer luck that these wolves found me. It'd only be a matter of time before the Silver Silence caught up to me.

Blood pumped in my ears so loud, it drowned out the sounds of their steps. Fire built in my core, dragging my Sage magic to the surface. It had been so long since I used my Sage magic that it flowed awkwardly for a moment but once it bubbled to the surface, I knew I was the true Sage. I planted my paws into the earth and released a long, deep growl.

I had left them. I renounced my title. Yet the magic remained. I would always be their Sage. I could still rule above all other alphas if I desired. It was time I reminded them of that.

The energy of magic built within me engulfing me with a static buzz standing my fur on end. I dug my paws into the earth and growled low. Every muscle tensed in preparation to charge. My magic burst from me as I pushed my aura toward the other wolves.

They immediately halted as the force of my magic hit them. They took a step back and looked at one another before tucking their tails between their legs and lowering their heads to me in submission.

I reined in on my magic just a little. Still, no one moved. As I walked amongst the wolves, I growled low. None tried to nip at me. They lowered their bodies to the ground and rolled over, exposing their underbellies. I could easily slay them right now.

Instead, I dug for information.

What is Amarok's plan? What does he want from me? I demanded from the wolves.

He wants your death, sire, one of them responded.

Why? I just want to be left alone. I will not interfere with pack business.

He is afraid of you. He knows you will stop his plans if you learn about them.

His plans?

He wants to grow the packs… the ancient way, another one told me.

My blood ran cold. He wanted to force lycanthropy on the humans. He would create an army of wolves who would go from village to village, raping and biting innocent women. He would force them to drink our blood to turn them. Bile crawled up my throat burning me from the inside.

Amarok was right to fear me, I told them.

S-sage? one of the wolves asked. His entire body shook as he spoke. *That's not the worst of it, sire.*

I turned to glare at the wolf at my paws.

He wants to take your mate for his own. He can hear her now and won't stop looking for her. We've… we've been trying to get to her but she's being protected.

Images of my mate in the arms of my enemy halted my breath. She smiled at his touch and willingly went to his bed. I swallowed down the nausea and turned my fear inward. Replacing her image with Amarok pleading for his life beneath my fangs, I growled. The world spun around me, blurring my vision. I could only hear the sounds of my heart beating in my head.

I didn't recognize my own voice when I barked at the wolves around me. *Who are you loyal to?*

You, my Sage, they all spoke together.

Go back to Amarok. Tell him nothing of this meeting, but keep me updated with his movements. This will all end soon. Be aware, those that choose his side will die along with him. Keep your noses down until I return.

I smiled, as I reached for my magic. The comforting warmth of my power had been buried deep within me when I deserted the packs. Pushing the magic towards the new wolves I placed a protection around each of them, so Amarok would not be able to influence them like before. I released them before I turned all of my attention toward Kassy.

I breathed deep, hoping to detect any trace of her. My focus shattered when I couldn't find her scent. My paws hardly touched the earth as I sprinted to the last place I had sensed her.

I practically leapt when I found her scent lingering on the fallen leaves. I buried my nose in the dirt, taking it all in. What I hadn't noticed the last time was the lingering traces of my sister. Kelly had been here as well. My sisters' musky scent had overpowered my mate's lighter aroma and had distracted me. I sorted through the fragrances and pulled out my mate's scent. I followed the trail until it mixed with a horse. She had taken off on Jericho, presumably toward the local village.

My breathing increased as I ran, and I slowed down only when I reached the edge of the woods. They'd kill me easily if I took one step closer. I called for Conri's consciousness in my mind. He was buried so deep in darkness that I grumbled as I carried his dead weight through the forest.

I circled the town, sniffing the air. She had been there only hours ago. Darkness painted the edges of my vision. The woods were not safe for her. As I encircled the town, I picked up her trail again, leading north. The scent of other men surrounded hers and I zeroed in on their direction, lusting for their blood. How dare they come so close to my mate.

The scent of the men disappeared as she headed deeper into the forest. My heart stopped. If any one of Amarok's wolves found her before me, they would drag her back to him and he'd take what he wanted, and leave her shredded.

She'd fight. She'd always fight. But would they kill her? I clenched my jaw at the thoughts of what they'd do to her if I didn't find her.

My paws tore at the earth as I ran ever faster toward my love. Her scent still lingered in my nose, driving me to pick up speed. I didn't stop moving once I caught her trail. I frantically tried to reach her before it was too late. My enemies wanted her, and I had to find her first. Even if she hated me, I had to keep her safe from those that only wanted to hurt me. Even if that meant I'd forever be her guard dog, lingering in the shadows. I'd do whatever it took to protect her.

Exhaustion threatened to overtake me when her scent vanished. And not just her scent but all scents. Even the earthy aroma of the forest disappeared. The very air evaporated from my lungs. I circled the spot I had lost her scent but found nothing. She was simply gone. I couldn't do this alone. I sighed and gave into the need to ask for help.

I pushed down my panic with deep, even breaths. Opening myself up to the magic within me, I called out for my sister. Kelly and the other wolves sat huddled in a cave. Stretching my mind out toward hers, I spoke mind to mind with my sister.

Kelly! I screamed for her. *Conri needs you.*

Fuck. Wolfe? Her words echoed bitterly in my head.

Yeah? Your candy-ass brother had a fucking panic attack and checked out.

What happened?

She saw us change and ran, and now he's pussing out. I had to take control before he got us killed.

He what? Your mate? I smelled you on her when I first saw her but... your true mate?

Why the fuck would I be so freaked if she were just a woman?

I...I saw her as a wolf in a vision when she touched me, but I didn't think....

The pack nearly killed us, but she saved us. I wanted to claim her the moment I knew, but he wouldn't let me. Fucking cock sucker said it had to be her choice. And now we're fucked. Amarok wants to turn humans against their will. Starting with her!

And what do you need me to do?

Fucking find her! Was I the only one that understood what this could mean? *She's a Hunter, but...I don't know...there's something more to her. If Amarok claims her, it will kill us. Even if she doesn't love me, he can't have her.*

Silence penetrated the bond between my sister's mind and mine.

Fuck. She dragged out the word. *What in the world is he thinking? This could destroy the packs!*

We agree. He needs to be stopped! We need you to find her and keep her safe. Send the others to us. We're going back. My chest tightened, and I had to fight to keep the meat in my stomach down. *Find her, sister. I'm begging you.*

You must love her. I have never heard you beg, Wolfe, she laughed.

Fuck. Of course, I love her, bitch! Why else would I be asking you for help? I need her. We cannot breathe without her. I'd find her myself if she weren't terrified of us. We need you to bring her back to us.

I loathed showing weakness to anyone, but Kelly was the worst. Conri wouldn't survive if Kelly didn't help us.

Please, I begged one last time before severing the connection

21
A Huntin' We Will Go
Scarlet

The sizzle of a frying pan woke me the next morning. I folded the blanket he had thrown over me last night and sat on the small stool, watching him. Despite his short height and enormous belly, he knew his way around the kitchen. He climbed onto a low stool, pulling down two colorful plates. He piled them high with potatoes fresh from his garden and eggs from his chickens out back.

"No meat?" I yawned.

"Nope." He handed me a plate as he sat next to me. "Want to come with me today to check my traps?"

"Sure." My mind drifted back to walking through the woods with Conri as we tracked our prey. I turned away from my Saba to hide the tears building up. "Not like I have anywhere else to be," I said to myself.

"And maybe you can tell me the real reason you are here?" He gave me a side eye as he ate his food.

I paused with my fork halfway to my mouth. "How is it you always know?" I raised an eyebrow at him. He practically raised me but I hadn't seen him in several winters.

"Your father always hated that, too." He grinned. "He would try to sneak out at night, but I could always find him."

I dropped my fork and stared at him. "That didn't answer my question."

"You have your secrets, and I have mine. Maybe if you tell me what's bothering you, I will tell you what you want to know." We ate our food in silence but inside my brain was racing. *Secrets. I'm so fucking tired of secrets.* If the price for his secrets were mine… I picked up my fork and shoved a mouthful in without saying another word.

I could leave now and go back to the hunt. I could bury my hurt and move on. But I know Saba would find me before I had gotten far. Besides, I was just as likely to get myself killed by how distracted I had become. I took a few more bites, then changed into fresh clothes before grabbing my boots. The leather was still warm from the fire as I slipped them over my chilly feet.

I threw my gear on my back, wrapped my red cloak around my neck, and waited for him by the door. Saba came out of his room wearing only light pants and a shirt. He carried a small pack on his shoulders as well, but I saw no weapons. My eyes scanned his body for where he hid his knives. I hadn't hunted with him since I was a little girl, and couldn't remember it well. It was Saba. He had his ways, so I just shrugged and opened the door for him.

Saba moaned and groaned as he made his way out of the cabin, yet the moment he entered the woods, he climbed over and around the trees like a child. We quickly came to his first snare, which was empty. He knelt down to reset it.

Finally, he broke the silence between us. "You ready to talk yet, kiddo?"

"I…I don't know."

"If you don't talk, I can't help you." He looked up at me, waiting.

"I know. It's complicated." I rubbed my arms, not wanting to look at him.

He stood, heading off to find another snare. I followed, watching the ground.

"Love usually is," he spoke lightly as we walked.

I stopped dead in my tracks. "I said nothing about love," I said a little too loudly.

"You didn't have to. It's written all over your face."

"I…I'm not in love. It's just…."

"If you don't love him, then why are you here?" He turned to look at me, one eyebrow cocked. "Kiddo, if you don't love him, then why are you hurting so much?"

"I…"

A lead weight settled in my gut, and I knew he was right. But we could never be. He was a wolf and I was a Hunter. What kind of life could we ever have? *Fuck!* His warmth wrapped around me like a blanket, and I wanted him even more than before, despite what he was. *No!* I scolded myself, and pushed Conri from my head.

"Come on, I think the next one is full." He motioned for me to follow, and he led us through the trees.

His words shook me from my thoughts. "How do you know?" I asked, but Saba just tapped his nose and gave me a little wink as he walked on.

I reached for my bow. I needed answers even if I had to force them. We walked in silence a little longer before he threw up his fist, clearly signaling me to halt. He turned to look at me. With one finger to his lips, he pointed off in the distance with his other hand.

I heard them before I saw them. Two small wolf cubs were pouncing on his snare. I knocked an arrow aiming at them.

Saba glared at me, shaking his head. I stared back before finally lowering my bow and watched them. They yanked and pulled at the rabbit until the snare finally snapped. They fought over the body as they ran off, each holding onto one half.

"Why'd you let them have it?" I hissed at him.

"They needed it more than I did," he said coolly.

"But they are just animals. They can find another."

"Not those two. Hunters killed their mother. They have no one to look out for them."

"How...." I stood with my hand on my hip. "How the hell could you know that?"

"Are you going to finish your story?"

"Are you going to finish yours?" I said through gritted teeth.

Saba glared back at me. "What truth are you hiding from me that hurts so much?" Saba practically yelled at me.

I had never seen Saba angry at anyone, let alone me. I gulped hard at his tone.

"I... He's..." I couldn't say it.

"A wolf," he finished for me.

My jaw dropped as I stared at him. How had Saba known the wolves could be men and not told anyone?

Every nerve vibrated within me, screaming at me to run but I pressed harder.

"Yes," I growled.

"And what is so wrong with that?" Saba's tone matched my fury.

"He's a beast!" I winced as the word left my mouth. "He lied to me." I continued in a lower tone. "He knew what he was, what I am, and he still let me fall in love with him. He never even told me the truth." I was sobbing now.

"Wolves are very secretive. And for good reason. They don't tell just anyone what they are. Especially Hunters." His face softened as he stepped closer to me.

"It doesn't matter. I don't care anymore. Let's get some meat already. I'm freezing." I wrapped my cloak tighter around me.

"Nock a bolt." He said and turned to walk off. I did as I was told and followed him.

We didn't walk far before he stopped again, crouched, and pointed in front of him. A large turkey waddled not fifty yards from us. I aimed my crossbow and pulled the trigger. My bolt struck him in the chest, and he fell instantly.

"Alright, now for your secrets." I demanded.

Behind his back, I stepped back to nock another bolt. He stood with a chuckle, walked over to the dead bird, and brought it back to where I stood.

This time, I aimed my bow at my Saba. He scoffed as he dropped the bird and rolled up one sleeve. He didn't even bother to look at me as I held my bow tight to my chest.

"Your parents lied to you all your life, kiddo." He knelt down on one knee. "After your friend died, your father kept you from me. He kept you from the truth. I'm sorry I have lied to you and for all the heartache and pain it has taken you to finally understand who you are." He looked down at his hand, and his fingers elongated and turned into furry claws.

I backed away until my back slammed into a tree.

How could I be so blind?

He sliced through the flesh of the turkey and gutted it with nothing but his hand… his claw.

My bow shook as I aimed. The once comforting weight of my weapon weighed down my arms as I held it upright. *Not my Saba.* I couldn't shoot the wolf in the forest even when she submitted to me. How the hell could I shoot my Saba. My aim lowered with each passing second.

"We are not all as bad as the wolf that killed your friend. And believe me when I say he paid for his mistake." He looked back at me like I was a child caught in the cookie jar again. "Put that down before you hurt yourself."

I lowered my crossbow, but I couldn't allow myself to release it.

"What—how?" My voice cracked.

"I am what others have called The Ancient One." Tears brimmed behind his eyes and my chest tightened watching his pain unfold before me. "I am the oldest living Were. Your grandmother left me when she learned the truth." He stood, wiping his eyes. "I lied to her. She didn't know what I was until after we were married, but by then she was already pregnant. The moment she gave birth to your father, she left us both."

He took another step toward me. I stepped back.

"Does that mean…." My eyes blurred.

"No. Your father's human. Simply sleeping with a werewolf won't turn a person. I never bit your grandmother, and even then, she would have had to drink from me. She never wanted any of that. The were must bite you and a blood exchange must occur."

I thought back to how close Conri had come to sleeping with me and wondered why he refused. *If simply fucking isn't enough to turn me, why did he resist?*

"It is next to impossible for a wolf not to bite their true mate during sex. Especially their first time." Saba answered my thoughts. "Your grandmother wasn't my true mate so it was easier for me."

I cocked my eyebrow. *And what of children?*

Saba chuckled. "Only a wolf pair can produce a Were child," he continued. "Your grandmother wasn't a wolf so naturally your father took after her. If I had wanted him to be a wolf, I would have had to have fed him my blood even before your grandmother fed him. He didn't find out what I was until after your friends' death. I had to tell him." Saba looked down at his feet. He looked so fragile for such a large man. Like Conri laying in that small bed. I gulped down the memories.

"They came for me. I had to keep you all safe." I recoiled at his news. The wolves had come for him, not Rose. She had died *because* of him. I gripped by bow tighter. "Before I met your grandmother, I was the Sage—the leader of all the packs. I knew if I stayed and brought her in with me, they'd either kill her or force the change, so I left to protect her. I tried to hide what I was, and it got her killed. When they found out what I had done, they hunted her, even though she didn't want to have anything to do with me by then." Saba leaned up against a tree for support. Tears now streaking his muddy face. "Your father still doesn't know that she's dead. I couldn't tell him."

He looked up at me with pleading in his eyes. "Conri didn't tell you because he thought he was protecting you. The wolves don't accept humans easily. But he loves you. If he didn't, he would have slept with you and left."

"I...I don't understand. Why are you telling me this now?" I dropped my bow. "Conri? How do you know his name? How do you know we didn't...?"

"Because I can tap into the minds of every wolf within a thousand clicks with little effort. Every once in a while, I let my shield down and listen. Magic has been running wild this past lunar cycle. There is untrained magic all around us, even now. I've been keeping my mind open to it. I think you are far past the time of learning the truth about your heritage. I know you haven't slept with him because I'd have smelt a change in you, and I don't."

I blushed at his words. The last thing I wanted was to talk about my sex life with my Saba.

"Besides, that's not something he'd likely do." Saba paused only to finish licking his paw clean before reverting it back to his human hand. I watched with wide-eyed curiosity. So many questions ran through my mind I couldn't focus on just one. "You're special, kiddo."

My curiosity peaked at his words as I stared at him.

"Royalty runs in your blood, kiddo. And probably a bit of magic, too. We belong to a very long line of Sages, all the way back to the beginning. When our family reigned, we were a peaceful people. When I left, the packs went wild. Conri did his best to pick up the pieces, but he has generations of anger that I gave the packs. He's broken. The packs are broken."

"He's the Sage now? You knew him?" I slumped to the forest floor.

"Yes, kiddo. When I left, I chose him to succeed me. Your mate is nearly as old as I am. Minus a few hundred cycles."

"Mate?"

He laughed. "I can smell it. You can choose to ignore it, but it will always be there." Saba's tone grew solemn again. He stepped closer to me and barely got out his next words. "He will never take another if you choose to walk away."

The weight of everything he said laid heavy on my shoulders suffocating me. I'd always been a lone human and now I had some kind of strange wolf magic running through me. Panic seized my heart in a vice and my vision blurred. I couldn't be some royal wolf human thing. No matter how much I loved my Saba… or Conri. I just couldn't deal with any of this.

"This is too much." I stood, throwing my bow over my back. "I can't." I started back to the cabin.

"You know where to find me if you need me," he shouted after me.

I practically ran back to the cabin. Mounting Jericho, I trotted off without a destination in mind.

22
McGowan
Wolfe

I paced the cave's entrance, waiting for the others my sister had sent to me. I needed to gather as many loyal wolves as I could before I faced Amarok. My sister was the alpha of her own pack, like the rest of my adult siblings, and she and her pack ran away when Amarok took the title of Sage for himself. When I left, the alphas should have voted on a new Sage, but Amarok used fear to steal the title and murdered anyone who might oppose him.

I dug at the hard rock for something to distract me. If Conri were here, he'd probably punch something. Yet he still retreated somewhere deep within me. If he didn't wake soon, it could ruin us. Conri was a true anomaly amongst the wolves. Most had accepted their wolf soon after their first shift. He still hadn't accepted me after three hundred winters. Conri's gentle nature wouldn't allow him to accept the fact that we are monsters inside. That we crave blood just as much as the next wolf. He never let me hunt when we were little. Not even for game.

We were never one. I was always Wolfe and he, the human. I ached to taste blood on my tongue every moment I was awake. Without Conri, I would rein terror over the whole of Breton. Even now, the chill of blood lust crept into my veins. If Conri didn't wake soon, I'd burn the world down to find and claim what's mine.

The rustle of the trees in the distance snapped me back to the reality at hand. The wolves stalked into view, connecting with my mind before I saw them completely. Two from my sister's pack walked into the cave.

It is us, Sage. We come to stand with you, Sullivan said.

I am glad you are here. I lowered my head slightly in a show of respect. It was something Conri would have done.

The wolves are running wild. Amarok has sent them in every direction, looking for you and is furious he can't find you, said Nolan, the youngest pack member.

Not just me, I growled.

They cocked their heads in confusion.

My sister hasn't told you? Amarok is planning on stealing my mate for himself before he lets the rest of the males loose on the humans. My blood ran cold just mentioning his plan.

My sisters' wolves lowered their heads and then their bodies until they lay flat on the ground.

We are with you, Sage. They pledged their allegiance to me with the ties of their magic.

I nodded once again. *Thank you. I appreciate your loyalty, and it is much needed if he is to be stopped.*

They stood, and Sullivan spoke again. *What can we do to assist you, my Sage?*

I need to get back to Madadh-Allaidh before his wolves find me. I will walk in on my own accord. But before I can do that, I need to know that my mate is safe.

All I could think about was Kassy, and I needed to know she was out of Amarok's reach.

Funny you should mention that... My sister's voice stopped my heart.

What happened? Where is she? My words came out harshly.

We found her, and she is safe for now. I lost her trail for a while but then out of nowhere I saw her emerge from the woods. Some kind of old magic had hidden her from me. She was with an old man, so I followed them. Something was strange about the man. It took me a while to put the pieces together. She paused, causing me to stop breathing. *It was so long ago that he left and I was just a pup then.... Wolfe, it was Sage McGowan. And she called him Saba. Your mate is royalty.*

I couldn't breathe. I couldn't think. She carried me, the largest wolf I've ever known, out of the woods alone. She didn't shy away from me when I was injured and delusional. Even my blood hadn't frightened this woman. No other woman could handle me at my worst, not even Kelly. Like some sort of cosmic gift, I had been mated to my mentor's granddaughter.

Our love had been written before I even knew her name.

Conri snapped back into our mind at Kelly's words.

What happened? he asked me sheepishly.

Hearing him broke me from my trance. *You fucking panicked and went to wherever the fuck you go when you puss out.*

The twins had one thing right: Conri had grown weak.

As much as I wanted to rush after Kassy, I had to circle around our little camp several times before heading out. Needing to cover our scent, we walked, backtracked, and then walked off again, all in different directions. We would have headed straight to where Kelly had said our mate was hiding if I thought I could, but that would lead Amarok right to her.

Where are we? What have you done? Conri asked when we were alone again.

Don't worry your pretty, little human head. We are safe. Far from the packs. And I found Kelly. She wasn't happy to talk to me, but she has done the impossible. I, the stronger one, had begged her to find my mate. His weakness was even affecting me.

Thank you. I'm sorry you had to beg her.

Fuck you! Keep out of my thoughts!

Um...I can't? As much as I hate you sometimes, you are me. So, fuck you. Why can't you ever ask Kelly nicely?

You know what happened last time we asked our brother nicely? We had to fucking kill him. What do you think would happen if Kelly saw your fucking weaknesses and challenged you? Do you think you could kill her, too? Fuck, even I don't think I could kill her.

She wouldn't.

Then you really are dumber than I thought. Why wouldn't she? If I keep her just a little afraid of me, then she won't. So don't you go fuck that up and be nice to her!

You're a dick.

Yeah, but I'm your dick. What would you do without me? Oh, wait…you'd be dead. So fucking wolf-up and move on. You're stuck with me, whether you like it or not.

We paced around a small clearing, scratching at our head and digging our nose into the dirt like it might rid us of the ever worsening headache.

Fuck you.

Fuck you, too. I could do this all day, but we need to keep moving before they find us again. You gonna puss out anymore, or what?

Seriously? Fuck you!

I laughed at him as we headed off in a new direction.

If you two are done bickering, I'd like to talk to my brother? Kelly's voice broke our fight.

Sister! I am glad to hear your voice!

What'd I say about being nice? I growled at Conri.

Conri, would you get a hold of Wolfe? He's getting tiresome.

I'll do my best. Thanks for finding our mate. Will you keep an eye on her until I get there? I need to make sure she's safe and see her one last time before I head back home.

I will, brother. Be safe!

Love to you, sister.

Conri was content to stay in the shadows as I held onto control. I could have marched him straight back to the packs, and he wouldn't have protested. But I needed him alive long enough to get Kassy to safety.

Keeping quiet again, are we? I goaded Conri, but still he was silent.

I had to do something to snap him out of his stupor, or we would die. When he let me go wild many winters ago after our lover was killed, he had been just as angry as I was. But this time, I sensed nothing from Conri. No emotions. Just an empty shell of a man within the wolf.

Come on, Conri. We'll find her first. I laid aside my spitefulness for a brief moment. *I need you, too.* I whispered hoping he wouldn't hear me.

A wolf that went rogue and lost all shreds of his humanity didn't last long. Huntsmen normally found the wolf and skinned him before the wolf even knew a Hunter was close.

What's the point? he finally responded. *Even when we find her…she hates us.*

She doesn't understand us. Once she does, she will come around.

He retreated back to his hiding place and grew silent.

Damn pussy.

Watch your mouth! said Kelly. My heart skittered as I heard her voice.

Sister! Where are you?

Watching her. She went on a hunt with the Sage and saw him shift.

She knows? Conri's voice came back to life. *Where is she? Have you spoken to her?*

Good to hear your voice, brother.

Fuck you, Wolfe spat, but I could hear the laughter in his voice.

Ignore him and answer me!

She knows what he is. She knows you're our Sage. She took off back to the woods. I am following her, waiting. She is scared. I can smell her fear.

Damn it.

We skidded to a halt and began pacing. Our breath was coming in quick bursts now as our heart slammed against our ribs.

Don't worry. I don't think it is hopeless. If it were, she would have gone home. I have to be careful, Conri. She is a Hunter. And from what I've heard, a damn good one.

That she is. Thank you for protecting her. It's not just her you have to watch out for. I'm sure Amarok's mutts won't be far behind. Be careful, sister!

You too, brother. The packs are all over the forests. They are looking for us all.

Love to you.

And to you, Brother.

Her mind faded from mine, and Wolfe and I were alone again.

I projected my thoughts to her wolves. *Go toward the mountains. I will meet up with you there. I have to find her and try to explain. If I can convince her, I will meet you in a few days' time. If not....* It was best not to think of what would happen if our mate refused us a second time.

Not one of them argued with me. To lose a mate was one of the worst things that could happen to a wolf, except, perhaps, losing a pup.

The weight in my chest lifted. She knew the truth. She might not have been ours yet, but our heart leapt at the hope that now bloomed within our chest. Our paws ran fast as we sped through the forest. Everything that happened now depended on if we could reach her before Amarok did.

23
Luna Sage
Scarlet

My heart raced as Jericho led me ever closer to Whitehaven. I had no desire to go home and face the commander of the Huntsmen, yet I couldn't steer my horse away. Instead, he slowed when we reached the little cemetery on the outskirts of town. I dismounted, leaving him to nibble off the last shreds of grass that remained. The snow would fall soon. Winter was near.

Slowly, I let my feet carry me to the tiny grave. There was one last stop I had to make before I could go any further. She was the reason I started my quest for vengeance in the first place. I'd lost so much since I lost her but at this moment she was all that mattered.

The icy breeze had nothing to do with my hands shaking at my side as I stood over Rose's final resting place. The smoky air floating from the chimneys nearby burned my nostrils. The smell instantly brought me back to the day she had died. Tears froze to my cheeks as I crumpled at her headstone.

"I am so sorry, Rose. I'm sorry I wasn't strong enough back then and now…" I looked down at my hands as they shook in the cold. Remembering Conri's fingers wrapped around mine brought the tears on faster. "I… I think I'm in love with one of them. But how could I be after what they did to you? To Nate?" I sobbed.

That day flashed back to my mind.

Her tiny arms swung at her side as she stood before me. "Come on, Kas. Come with me." I hesitated at the edge of the village and shook my head. "Nate's there." She prodded me.

"I… I can't." I told her and ran back home.

One small moment changed my entire life. I should have gone with her. It was a simple thing… If only I would have walked with her to her grandmother's house, she might still be alive, but I had been too afraid. By the time I gained the courage to follow her it had been too late. Her tiny body lay in my arms, bleeding and broken as she took her last breath.

After she died, I bottled up that fear and hatred and unleashed it on the wolves.

Nothing made sense now. I clung to the grass and buried my face over her final resting place. I let out every tear I'd been holding back for the past twenty winters.

The weight of her tiny body filled my arms once more and her warm blood trickled onto my lap as I held her. The tangy aroma brought acid to my throat. I gasped for breath.

"Rose," I cried at the image in my arms.

A snap of a twig tore my gaze from her and back to the surrounding forest. I gasped as her image now stood before me. The hazy figure was not quite corporeal, yet her eyes burned into me as if my old friend truly knelt beside me. My heart leapt at seeing my old friend yet fear at the ghost before me froze me in place.

"Rose!" I yelped, toppling backward at the sight of her. Her body was whole again and gone were the tattered remains I had stumbled over as I ran to find her. She wore the long, white dress her mother had buried her in and her hair hung loose over her shoulders. My breathing slowed as I realized it really was her. I sighed at her perfect image. She truly stood with me in my darkest moment.

"It's time to stop blaming yourself. My death was not your fault," her small voice spoke into the wind.

"I should have gone with you. I'm sorry." My words barely escaped my lips between the sobs I couldn't rein in.

"Then you would lay next to me." She knelt before me. "You also can't keep blaming the wolves. They are not all at fault. One wolf took my life. He had gone mad, but not all are like he was."

"But..."

"No. You cannot blame an entire group of people for one wolf's decisions. I may appear to be a small child, but I have roamed this world as long as you have, and I've seen things only a spirit could. I have seen much and know more than you think. Your grandfather has been a significant influence on me."

I cocked my head at my old friend's image.

She laughed. "Saba is much more than he seems. He can communicate with the spirits of those who have gone before. I was lost for a long time after my death. I wandered through the trees, looking for someone who could help me. I needed a guide, and I found him in the woods one day. He pulled me back from the edge of insanity. His kind aren't the monsters that fairytales would have us believe, Kas."

My heart stopped at hearing my old nickname from her. This really was my old friend, not just my imagination.

"Why haven't you come to me before?" I desperately needed my old friend again. "Why hasn't Nate?" I whispered.

She shifted so she sat cross-legged in front of me. "Nate loved you, and he knew you'd have to move on, so he did too." She sighed. "Besides, taking this form requires a lot of energy. I have watched you grow strong and brave, but ever so lonely. Don't let your fear stop you from love." She leaned in and brushed her hand across my cheek. Her touch was there, but it wasn't. A cold chill ran down my spine, then she was gone.

"Rose, I miss you," My words hung in the air, spoken to nothing but the cold headstones around me.

I miss you too, Kas. Her words echoed deep within me.

I sat there sobbing onto Rose's grave. Everything that ever mattered to me was gone, and I might as well lay on the cold hard earth until I joined my friend in whatever lay after.

My Saba was a wolf, and he hadn't told me until long after I'd become Scarlet. I'd hated the wolves all my life. How did anyone expect me to change that? I wanted my life back. I was happy in my old life. Sure, I was lonely, but I knew my purpose. Now…. Had I killed my own family? Was there the blood of distant cousins on my hands?

And Conri. My love was a wolf, and I could do nothing to change that. Was I responsible for the death of my mate's family? I couldn't say for sure. I had lived my life believing wolves were soulless, rabid creatures. The guilt overwhelmed me as I buried my head in my hands. I didn't want to think about it anymore, but I couldn't push it away. I couldn't go home, and I couldn't go back out and hunt. I had turned my back on Conri. I couldn't even go back to Saba after the way I treated him.

Something rustled behind me, causing me to jump to my feet. I turned around, looking for the source of the noise. I pulled my crossbow off my back and nocked a bolt. A flash of dark fur flew past my line of sight, and my eyes darted around to follow it. I took a deep breath before searching again. A wolf walked out of the woods toward the small graveyard where I stood.

My heart jumped to my throat. The massive wolf's lips curled into a snarl as it stalked toward me. My hands shook as I raised my bow to him then hesitated when three more wolves followed him out of the woods and surrounded me.

I steadied my breathing, aimed for the closest wolf, and pressed down on my trigger. The smaller wolf dodged just as the arrow released.

"Shit," I whispered and reloaded.

I followed their movements and this time my aim was on point. My arrow buried deep in the chest of the smallest wolf, dropping his body to the ground. The other wolves snarled in response.

I reached around to grab another arrow from my quiver and found it empty.

"Shit, shit, fucking shit." I backed away, keeping my eyes on the wolves.

A low growl from behind me stopped my heart. I was surrounded. I closed my eyes and waited. The brush of a body against my side snapped my eyes open again.

The white wolf walked past me and toward the others. She didn't hesitate to lunge for the largest of the wolves and clamped down on his neck. The other two wolves froze as the white wolf bled their leader.

I knelt, digging the knife in my boot out and crept forward.

The other wolves slowly circled the white one as she dropped the body of the big wolf. The white wolf had saved my life. The least I could do was watch her back. I jumped on one of the wolves as it stalked toward the white wolf.

It thrashed but I held on tight to its fur. I yanked my body to the side pulling the wolf to the ground. My legs straddled the beast as his paws tore at my arms. Pain throbbed through my arms as blood poured from the scratches. I pushed past the burning and with one hand I grabbed the monster's paws and with the other plunged my dagger into his throat. I twisted the knife and held on until he stilled.

When I finally caught my breath and looked up, I saw the white wolf staring at me. She sat next to the two wolves she had killed, her chest now coated in blood. She wasn't half as large as the wolf Conri had become but the longer I watched her the clearer it was she was the same one who submitted beneath my bow that day in the woods. She stood and pranced with gracefulness around the dead wolves toward me.

Panic rose in my chest. What did this wolf want with me? Why had she submitted to me and why had she saved me just now? Would she kill me or turn me? I didn't know. My heartbeat out of desperation for more time. My brain struggled to comprehend what was happening but my body reacted.

I rolled over to my knees and flung my knife at her. The wolf moved just as the blade left my hand. The knife struck her through her front arm. She whimpered and staggered back but didn't run.

"Shit."

I dropped my head and stood. I kept my eyes down and my hands raised in front of me as I approached.

She never looked me in the eye. Instead, the closer I got, the lower her head bowed. An injured wolf normally attacked, but she laid fully to the ground and submitted. Her whimper grew quiet as I reached for her.

"Hush, now." I tried to soothe her. Now what? I couldn't kill something that so willingly would let me, but she was a wolf.

Slowly, she raised her head, licking my face. I looked down at her in shock, and she quickly bowed her head.

"Fine." I sat on the ground and scooted toward her. "Don't bite me." I gripped her paw and yanked the blade from her leg. I probed the wound. "I don't think it's broken. You should be alright. The silver from the blade seems to have seared the skin so you won't bleed. But just in case..." I pulled a bandage out of my pack and wrapped her leg up. "There. That should keep it clean and help you heal." She nudged my hand with her muzzle. I couldn't help but laugh as I scratched her between her ears.

Conri chose well, a voice echoed in my head.

"What?" I jumped back.

Conri chose his mate well. He's been looking for you, Luna Sage.

"How can I hear you? Where is he?" I stared at her. "What did you call me?"

You are Conri's mate, Luna Sage. We can all hear each other. As for where he is, I cannot say, but you can. She stood tentatively on her injured leg. *If you open your heart to him as he has opened his to you, you'll find him. He loves you, Luna Sage. He weeps for your loss and searches for a way to bring you back to him.*

But how? How can I ask him to forgive me? How can I ask any of them to forgive me for all I have done? I thought to myself.

A look of understanding seemed to cross over her face. She nuzzled at my hand. *If you can forgive him, perhaps he can forgive you.*

The white wolf walked off the way she had come, leaving me pondering her words. She was right. I had to forgive Conri. We had to forgive each other for everything we'd done.

"I am sorry about your leg!" I shouted after her.

A small price to pay for my Sage.

I watched as the last bit of white disappeared into the trees then stood, staring after the wolf. "Luna Sage," I repeated. My Saba had said nothing about a Luna Sage. *What does that even mean?*

Find him. The wolf's voice echoed in my head.

A lightness filled me now at the thought of Conri. My heart rate slowed, and my breathing steadied. I now understood why Saba and Conri had kept their secrets.

They were protecting themselves and the families they left behind. They did nothing I wouldn't have done. How could I be angry at them for being themselves? Could Conri be angry at me for my own fears?

Reality sunk into my skin like the warmth of a blanket. The truth was, I loved him more than I'd ever loved anyone. The memory of the image I saw when I touched the white wolf flooded my mind. It was Conri's wolf and somehow, I just knew that the other wolf was me. The wind breezed through my hair, and I could picture myself running through the forest as a wolf side by side with Conri's wolf.

The ache in my chest I'd grown accustomed to lifted and joy pranced about my body. I knew in my bones as much as he had that he was my mate. Every bit of my soul called to his. I needed him to survive. All the fear and anger I'd had toward him shifted to those hunting him… hunting us… and fire lit behind my eyes. I'd burn the world down to find him and keep him safe.

I knelt to pick up my knife. The instant I touched the silver blade, it burned my skin. I dropped it and examined my fingers, but the small red lines faded quickly. I pulled a glove out of my pack and slid my hand into it. I picked up the knife with my gloved hand and touched the tip with my other. My skin sizzled as the silver seared my fingertips.

I dropped the blade and doubled over with nausea. *I wasn't…I couldn't be.* Conri hadn't bitten me, and we didn't have sex, so why did the silver burn?

You're not. Not yet, but he has claimed you. The wolf's voice echoed in my head. *Find him. Either way you choose, you must go to him.* With those words, she severed our connection, and disappeared completely.

24
Acceptance
Scarlet

I straightened, staring at the knife that lay on the ground and knew that I stood on the precipice of a life altering decision. My brain—that was taught to fear the wolves my entire life—told me to run away but my heart needed to find him and make up for a lifetime of wrongs. It didn't take long for me to make the choice that I knew there was no coming back from. Every bit of my soul was drawn to him, and I couldn't breathe without knowing if he wanted me, too.

Carefully, I picked up my equipment, and trudged back through the cemetery.

Find him, she had told me. But how? Open my heart to him. "Damn wolves and their riddles."

Jericho bucked the second I came into view.

"Shhh. It's me, boy." My voice soothed him, and he allowed me to mount him. Together, we trotted off.

"Open my heart," I reminded myself. I closed my eyes and let Jericho guide me. I breathed in the forest and smelled rain. Petrichor. Conri. My mate. He was looking for me like I was him. I sighed happily at the mental contact.

My vision shifted to the first time I saw Conri, injured in the woods. That was a lifetime ago. I was afraid when I first saw him, but…if it had only been fear of him, I would have left him there to die. No, there was something more in that memory that pushed me toward him. Fear had flashed in *his* eyes. He was more afraid than I was, but not of me or of those hunting him. His fear was far deeper than that. Like he'd been running his entire life but the moment his eyes met mine…

I shivered. When our eyes met all those weeks ago, we were one. I tied myself to him in that single moment as surely as he had, and we both had been pushing down our desires to protect the other.

I'd hide no longer. Taking a deep breath, I steadied my nerves. A rush of heat ran through me, and my heart caught in my throat. *He. Is. Mine.* I claimed him. Even though I was alone in the woods far from him, I claimed him. And I'd tear apart any creature that stood in my way to get to him.

Tears flowed down my cheeks and around the smile on my lips. I could see him. Or rather, I was seeing through his eyes, and he through mine. His wolf had been running, but the moment my heart connected with his, he—we—slid to a stop.

Our hearts beat as one. A deep rumble echoed through his body and rang in my ears. Though he was leagues away, it was as if I had been the one making the sound.

He huffed and started running with more vigor. I nudged Jericho forward, and we ran. The earth shifted, and I was back in my own body, but I still sensed his lingering mind like a tether. My thighs tightened around the horse's ribcage as I urged him on. My breath turned ragged, and my heart beat out of my chest.

Conri

We clung to the hope that we still had a chance to explain ourselves. Small as it was, we needed that hope to push us forward and drive us faster. Our pulse thrummed in our ears as we ran. We sniffed the air, searching for her scent.

We need to find her. Wolfe's voice was barely audible over our heartbeat.

For once I didn't argue with him but ran faster. Amarok wanted her, but we'd never allow that to happen. We would always stand between her and anyone who would do her harm. Even if she hated us, we'd watch over her and keep her safe.

Wolfe and I agreed on this. We would abandon everything to keep our mate from the fate Amarok would have for her.

The mud under our paws squelched as we ran, coating our legs in sludge. Our tongue flopped from our muzzle, tasting the musty air. Fear gripped us when we sensed them in our mind. More and more wolves had left the safety of Madadh-Allaidh and they were heading for the human lands.

Magic coursed through us, urging our muscles faster. They were coming for her. The images of what he would do to her if he got a hold of her flashed through our mind, slamming us to a halt. We howled in rage at the thought of him touching a single hair on her head.

Our sister's mind flooded into ours, calming us. *Calm your heart, brother. She will never find you this way.*

Find me? Where is she?

She is safe. We had a little run in with a small pack, but she is safe. And hopefully looking for you, but she can never find you in this state. Calm yourself and open your heart to her.

How? The forest spun around us. Our vision blurred. We had to close our eyes to keep from getting sick.

Stop thinking so much, Conri, and just feel. It might hurt, but it will be worth it. I love you, brother.

Kelly's presence vanished from our mind as fast as she had slammed into it. We rubbed our paws on our face. Breathing deep through our snout, we smelled her. Her scent had led us injured and afraid straight to her that night. She had saved us. We breathed deep, remembering her tender touch as she tended to our wound.

Her soft lips pressed into ours as we laid half-conscious, unaware of our actions. Wolfe had claimed her the moment he saw her. I had pushed him away for so long that I couldn't see how much he had protected and guided me all my life. He had been the one to push us forward after our mother's death. He had fought our brother and kept us from losing that fight. He had saved our family when others had challenged them. He may be an arrogant asshole, but he loved our family as much as I had and that included Kassy now.

I had pushed him away for so long but at this moment, I loved him. He had claimed our mate when I was too blind to see her for what she was.

It had taken me over three hundred winters to see that he was me, and I was him. I embraced the side of myself I never thought I'd accept, and finally Wolfe and I were one. Everything clicked into place, and I saw clearer than I ever had. Colors popped brighter. My hearing increased tenfold, and my sense of smell went wild. I howled in satisfaction. There was only one piece left to make me whole.

Her scent grew stronger, inviting me to follow. My paws dug into the surrounding mud, launching my body into a sprint. My heart practically leapt from my body, and I smiled. Her face flashed into my mind, slamming me to a stop again.

As her mind joined mine, I shifted my eyes and focused on what I saw around her. Trees surrounded the back of a horse's head. Her heart raced at our connection, and she nudged her horse into a run.

I growled at the pleasure of her mind tied to mine. She urged her horse faster as she ran toward me, not away. My paws nearly floated off the ground as I ran toward my mate. Somewhere along the way, our connection broke, but her pull still guided me straight to her.

My body halted as I heard her horse approach. Her aroma hardened my cock the instant I smelled her, and I used all my strength to stay put and not startle Jericho the moment she came into view.

25
Mated
Scarlet

*J*ericho had never been so close to a wolf before, and Conri's imposing form was a force to be reckoned with. Jericho bucked and reared . My grip on the horse slipped and my back hit the ground, forcing the air from my lungs. I saw Jericho's tail flash in the distance as he ran from the perceived danger.

I struggled for air as the world spun for a moment, but nothing would stop me from reaching him. The last time his wolf bowed to me, I ran. Not today. Today, I would stand tall. Today, I would stay. Rolling over to my stomach and pushing myself up onto my knees, my eye met his. He sat in front of me perfectly still, not daring to move.

"I'm sorry," I said with all the strength I could muster.

He leaned in and licked my face. I laughed, throwing my arms around his thick, wet fur. My body relaxed into him as his warmth spread over me. I had found him and would do everything to keep him.

His whimpers pulled me away from him. Time passed slowly as I watched as the wolf contorted and his whines turned to cries as the human emerged. He lay there in silence, breathing heavily to catch his breath. My heart in my throat as I waited for his reaction.

Finally, Conri knelt naked in front of me, gasping. My hands hung in the air between us as I hesitated to reach for him. His arms didn't hesitate and he encircled me, pulling me close to him as he nuzzled his nose into my neck and breathed deep.

"You came back," he whispered against my neck. I welcomed the tickle of his scratchy beard against my skin.

"I had to. I needed to. Conri, I..." My breath caught in my throat. Would he truly forgive me?

"I love you, Kassy." His words floated in the air between us.

"I love you, too," I sobbed in relief.

If I could hear the other wolf, I'm guessing you can hear me now? I asked.

His chest rumbled with laughter. *Yes, I can hear you, and you can hear me. Thank you for not killing my sister.*

I pulled away. "Like your sister-sister?"

"Yes, my sister. She's my Lieutenant. I sent her to find you." He pulled me toward him again and rained kisses on my eyes, nose, and then gently pressed his lips to mine. "I have lived so long, I thought I would never find my true mate." He wrapped his hands in my hair. "We wolves only have one true mate in our lifetime." His lips pulled the air from my lungs the moment they connected with mine. "You are mine," he breathed. "I am yours, and we shall never have another."

Conri pulled me into his lap, and I wrapped my legs around his waist.

"You sure are happy to see me." I laughed, grinding my hips against his hardened cock. Heat settled deep in my core, begging to have him.

"You have no idea." He nuzzled against my neck. "Kelly told me your Saba was my old Sage. So, you know what happens if we…"

I shoved him backwards onto the ground and stood over him. A look of confusion passed over his face as I tossed my bow and pack to the side. His expression changed to that of hunger as I dropped my cloak and slowly unbuttoned my shirt and tossed it to the ground. He licked his lips, reminding me of that morning at the shooting range. I took another step back as I slowly stepped out of my boots and then my pants.

Once more, I was naked before him.

I couldn't tell if the growl came from him or me. I placed one foot on either side of his hips.

"Yes. I spoke to my Saba." I placed my hands on my hips. "I know everything."

Conri sat up to kneel in front of me and grasped my ass in his hands, pulling me into him. I dug my nails into his hair and sighed as his hot breath lingered against my skin. His lips kissed my stomach as he moved his hand between my thigh, parting my legs The air was cool against my skin, but my core burned hot as a forge. He stroked the length of my leg with his fingertips as his mouth lowered and I yanked his hair hard as he teased me. Every nerve lit up, vibrating throughout my body when he flicked his tongue over my clit. I pulled his face into me, demanding more. His hand moved to my slit, twirling his fingers in my slickness.

"Conri," I moaned as I leaned on him for support.

A low, satisfied growl left his lips, but it didn't stop his tongue from teasing me as I dug my nails into his scalp. He thrust two fingers inside me while his other hand gripped my ass as his nails scored my flesh. The droplets of blood dripped down my ass, and it only pushed me closer to the edge of release as he worked in and out of me.

You taste so fucking delicious," he growled.

"Hum," I moaned.

"Are you going to cum for me?" he asked as he nibbled at my clit.

"Yes," I whimpered.

"Let me hear you."

"Yes, Conri. I'm going to fucking cum."

"I want to taste it." His mouth crashed against me and he sucked at my clit until my legs shook and a tidal wave of pleasure washed over me.

"Fuck me!" I screamed out in pleasure.

He lifted my legs laying them over his shoulders as he held me tight to his face. I rocked against him as I rode the wave back down. He laid me gently to the forest floor and licked me clean before crawling on top of me.

He left me gasping, but I was far from done. I lowered my hand to his shaft and stroked it gently, twirling the tip around my fingers. He closed his eyes and tilted his head.

"Wait," he breathed. I looked up at his face. His wide eyes looked at me in alarm. "Are you certain? We do this, and there's no going back. I won't be able to stop Wolfe from taking you fully." He stroked my face with the soft pad of his thumb. "It could kill you or make you one of us. Forever." His eyes glossed over with tears.

I smiled and wrapped my legs around his hips and flipped him over to his back. He grinned slightly but the fear didn't leave his face.

There was no choice. There never had been. I had always been his, and he had always been mine.

I stood and walked to the knife on the ground and pulled it from the sheath. His eyes doubled in size at the dagger in my hand. I stood over him, straddling his hips.

"I'm certain," I gasped as I took the knife in my hand and dragged it from my shoulder to my clavicle. Pain mixed with pleasure urging me on.

His eyes flashed a bright golden hue and his hands shifted into paws and back again but he held himself firmly to the forest floor.

I dropped the knife and ignored the sting from the cut as I knelt above him. Reaching my hand between us I guided his shaft to my center.

"Are you certain you want to be tied to me?" I asked as I rubbed his cock in my wetness.

He growled, grabbed my hips and drove me onto his shaft in one swift motion. I gasped as his cock slammed into me. The force of his thrust threw me forward and my breasts rubbed against his chest.

His eyes moved to the bleeding wound at my neck, and he sat up, pulling me with him. I wrapped my legs around his back as I ground against him. I leaned into him, giving him access to my cut. His lips found my neck and lapped at the blood.

A deep groan rumbled against my body as he drank me in. I rocked my hips to his, harder and faster watching his fangs grow and nick my skin.

My name spilled from his lips as he pulled me off him. Watching his face coated in my blood brought new dampness between my legs.

His eyes scanned me, looking for any trace of regret.

Last chance. His words were a soft caress in my ear.

I reached for him, letting my thumb graze his fangs. "Oh, Conri. My gorgeous wolf." I pushed his hand against his lips and nodded.

Conri sank his fangs into his own arm, then brought it to my lips. Dark blood seeped from the punctures.

I licked my lips before wrapping them around his wrist. Warmth spread over my body as I drank from him. Swallowing down the hot liquid filled my head with a buzz stronger than any alcohol ever had. His cock twitched inside me as I drank. His eyes rolled to the back of his head. I rocked my hips, grinding my clit against the curly hair at the base of his cock. I bit down harder as the pleasure built within me.

The moment he pulled his arm away, an intense pleasure pulsed throughout my body. Every fiber of my being stood apart from the other. He pulled out of me, leaving me wanting.

"Turn around," he ordered.

I turned around and knelt on all fours, parting for him. His massive hands gripped my hips as he plunged his cock inside.

My senses were heightened, and I was keenly aware of where his cock was inside me. Every move he made. Every thrust. Even the tiny hairs on his legs brushing against mine. He leaned over me, palming my breast and his thumb flicked over the hard nub.

"Oh, fuck, Conri," I moaned.

"Kassy." He spoke so tenderly. "My gods, Kassy, I'm so fucking close."

I turned my head to look at him. His golden eyes shined brighter than the crescent-moon shone through the trees. He lit up the forest with his glow. As the pleasure burst from my core, colors lit up around me like never before. The trees were no longer brown but auburn, walnut, cinnamon, and chocolate. Stars I had never been able to see before were suddenly shining down on us.

Conri groaned as he pulled my hips into him harder and faster.

"Fuck, Kassy. Gods, you feel so fucking good."

"Conri," I moaned as I came.

"Fuck," he screamed. "Your tight little pussy... fuck me..."

"Cum for me, Conri. I need you to cum inside me."

He groaned. "Fuck." He thrust one last time before sliding gently out of me and flopping to his side.

Conri pulled me down to the ground with him, kissing me softly. We lay facing one another on the ground. Every hair on my arms stood as he gently stroked my back. He brushed the hair off one side of my neck. His lips caressed the skin behind my ear. Moving to the wound that had nearly healed, he licked the rest of the blood away.

Every nerve cried out for more.

He cupped my breast in one hand, sliding the other to the apex of my thighs. His fingers twirled around my clit as he massaged my breast. I buried my face in my arms, moaning his name.

"Conri." I gasped.

I pulled my hips away for just a second.

"I need more." There was no hesitation in my voice. "Don't be gentle."

Conri pinched on my nipple and smacked my ass before he rolled on top of me.

"Are you sure you want me to play rough?" his husky voice whispered in my ear.

I pulled my hair away from my neck and barked, "Do it!"

He pulled my legs up over his shoulders. I had to lift myself to my elbows to reach him. He slammed his cock into me as his fangs sunk deep in my calf muscles, and my pussy tightened with pleasure.

His fangs bit down harder as his dick nearly cleaved me in two.

"Fu-fu-fuck." Blood spilled over my lips where my teeth dug in.

"Not yet." He slowed his pace as he licked my leg clean. "I want to remember this moment." He lowered my legs back to the forest floor and leaned over me. His fingers brushed over my lips before he kissed them. "Fuck, Kassy. Even your blood tastes delicious." He licked the crimson liquid from my mouth.

"Conri," I sighed, pulling him into me. "I can't..." Everything tingled. Even my lips grew numb. "Make me cum." I begged.

He locked eyes with me and thrust in and out of me harder and faster. I dug my fingers into his back drawing blood.

"Fuck," he screamed through gritted teeth.

"Cum for me," I pleaded.

His grunts grew louder as my core clenched around him.

"Kassy," he moaned as he came.

Slowly he pulled out, laying down beside me on the ground. I rolled over to my side and crawled into his arms. He traced my spine with his fingertips as I struggled to catch my breath.

I leaned in to kiss his lips. "Worth the wait."

A satisfied smile spread across his mouth as he kissed me again, exploring my mouth with his tongue. I would never grow tired of his kiss.

We laid under the moon and stars in silence for a long time, content to simply hold each other. He was all mine and I his. He was a wolf, and I was his mate. Our blood mixed and we became one. About a million questions ran through my head and I struggled to settle on just one.

"Now what?" I asked. I knew it was vague, but I was too scared to ask what was truly on my mind. *Would I die?*

"For you? Whatever you want." He kissed my nose, ignoring the heart of my question. "We can go wherever you want. We can run from the packs or go back to them. I leave it up to you, my mate. But if we go back, it will mean a fight. Amarok has called me to endure the Trials. It will not be pretty or easy, but I think I would survive if you were with me."

"The Trials?" I asked, welcoming the distraction from the change we both knew was coming.

"It's been a long time since we've held a Trial, but it's basically a test of loyalty but in the most barbaric way." He brushed his fingertips over my face.

"Will we be safe from them if we ran? I've already been attacked once?"

He sat up on his elbow and looked at me. "Honestly, I doubt it. Amarok is after more than just me." He swallowed hard. "I... I hesitate to tell you this but... He wants you for his own. I don't even think you'd be safe if we went back to face the Trials."

"What if you win? What if we kill him?"

"His death would solve a lot of problems." He laid down on his back and pulled me into his arms.

I laid there looking up at the stars.

Finally, I broke the silence. "Your sister called me Luna Sage." I laid my leg over his. "What does that mean?"

"She did, did she? I will have to scold her for that. I would have liked to have been the one to tell you just how special you are." He ran his hand up my leg. "In our world, there are few females, and even fewer that are strong enough to be an Alpha, let alone a Sage. You have Sage magic flowing in your veins. I'm pretty sure you are even stronger than me." His fingers brushed my hips, sending a shiver down my spine. "But for you it means whatever you want. I'm the Sage, and I rule over all the wolf packs. If you choose, we can rule together. If you don't, it means nothing." He gripped my inner thigh tight. "We haven't had a Luna Sage in a long time. Your great-grandmother was the last one. She, too, was a wolf by choice."

My grandmother had left because of what my Saba was, yet his mother had chosen this life. I wasn't sure how to process that, so I tried to push it aside for the moment. I had too many other questions to get through.

I fired the worst of my thoughts at him all at once before I could think better of it to ask. "Apparently, I am far younger than you. What will the packs think of that? Not to mention that I am a Hunter. When will we know if this will kill me or turn me?"

"First, do you plan on killing any more of us?" His fingers traveled up, tangling in the hair between my legs. I pushed the worry down to answer his question.

"No, not unless they try to hurt you." I thought about it for a moment. "I've only ever wanted peace, even if that means brokering a truce between the humans and the wolves."

Conri growled in satisfaction at my words. My pussy clenched at his growl.

"Then that no longer matters. Because you are my mate, you will control your wolf better than most pups, so your age won't matter either."

"And the killing me?" I hesitated to ask.

"I…" He kissed my lips gently. "It'll take a while for our blood to mix. I want to lie here with you before it fully takes hold. It takes longer for some and quicker for others. My venom is strong so… I fear it won't take long, my love. I'm sorry."

"Will it hurt?" My voice shook as I asked the thing I feared the most.

He moved his hand to stroke my face before answering me. "All change comes with a little pain. So yes, my love, it'll hurt. But I won't leave your side." His face winced as if remembering his first shift.

"What about my wolf? What about yours? Can I talk with him?"

"Your wolf is an extension of yourself. I've struggled with Wolfe because we are so different, but losing you showed me that we aren't as different as I thought. I'm sure once you turn, he will be anxious to meet you. As far as your wolf is concerned... You're stronger than I am and more confident. I'm sure you won't have any issues with her."

I thought back to everything that happened to me when I joined the Huntsmen. From the man in the shower, to my knife in his chest, to Nate, and to the wolves I killed. The pain of that time was still buried deep within me, but it made me stronger and so would the next phase of my life.

Emotional pain was far different than physical pain though, so I changed the subject. "What does a Sage do, really?"

"Each pack has its own alphas that control their wolves. I control the alphas."

"Saba told me that when he reigned, the wolves were more peaceful. What happened?"

"When he left, he tore a hole in the packs. Your grandmother wasn't his true mate so some of the wolves were angry that he chose a human over his own kind. Others understood he chose love." He looked away. "I think if your grandmother knew the truth before, she might have kept him from leaving the packs. I think the packs needed her."

"Do they need me?"

He sat up on his elbows and kissed my face. "I need you."

I glared at him. "Nothing but honesty from here out," I demanded of him.

"Okay… Honestly>Yes. I think the packs need you and I think the packs were strongest when your great-grandmother and then your grandfather ruled." He kissed me again. "Let's face it. When it's just a male ruling, we get fucking wild and violent. I think a powerful female is just what the packs need." He sat up, offering me a hand. "If you will have us, that is."

I laced my fingers with his and kissed the back of his hand. "I will."

I barely got the words out before the searing pain had me clamping my jaw. I writhed on the ground as every muscle in my body sizzled like a steak in a frying pan. Conri gripped my arm tightly.

"Breathe, Kassy. Just breathe through the pain."

I gulped. "Trying," I squeaked out.

"It'll only last a moment. You're strong, Kassy. You can make it, but you must remember to breathe."

The heat spread throughout my body, burning my lungs. The coppery-tinged aroma hit my nose, sending my stomach into convulsions. Conri placed his hands on my back and turned me to my side. Pulling my knees to my chest, I retched what little food I had managed to consume the last few days all over the ground before me. Conri stroked my back as I shook violently.

"I…can't…." I tried to say, but the sounds of his whimpering stopped me. Something warm and furry nuzzled up to my back.

Take what you need from me. My strength is your strength.

My body tingled with the flow of magic from the wolf at my back. I thought of his strength the first time he laid in that tiny bed, curled up against me, and my muscles relaxed, and my breathing steadied. I rolled over to see Conri's wolf beside me.

Thank you, my mate.

He licked my face, and the last of the burning washed away. I heard her within me but as if from underwater. She was wild and untamed, but not yet strong. Her presence reminded me of myself before Rose had died. I'd run free through the forest and climb to the top of the trees. Slowly, she grew strong within me, but I still dominated her. I knew she needed to run. She called to be set free, but I couldn't give her full control yet. The image of the ivory wolf from the vision I shared with Kelly burst forth and she howled again to be released. I trembled at her strength then finally bowed to her, letting Ivory come forth and join me as one.

The pain returned once more as my joints twisted and my muscles mutated. Whimpering at my strain, my mate edged closer. Fur coated my naked flesh, and I became as he was.

I stood to face my mate.

You are beautiful. He bowed low before me. His body tensed as he scanned the forest, then relaxed as he looked back at me.

So are you, my mate. I spoke to his mind. Ivory's approval radiated out of me as I stepped up to him and nuzzled his neck.

A strange tingle flowed from my body and wrapped around his. His pride welled up inside me as if it were my own. Mixed with that pride, his heart rate increased and his muscles tensed. Before I could ask, he laughed.

Your magic is strong. He smiled. *A Sage bond.*

I cocked my head.

Your magic has bonded with mine. Now, no matter where you go, we will sense each other. We are bonded, stronger than any two have ever been.

His emotions flipped back and forth so much I finally paused to sort through them. I calmed my mind and focused my ears on the forest around us. Snorting and scratching sounds came from my left, and I snapped my head in that direction.

What is it? I asked. Ivory growled deep within me as I fought to keep her at bay.

Too far out still. A deer maybe?

I sensed the lie burning his throat and the unfamiliar sensation pushed me to turn and face the danger.

Only honesty. Remember. Ivory's anger got the best of me, and I snapped at Wolfe, nicking his tail.

Fine. He growled and turned to stand beside me. *Bigger than a deer, I think.*

He raised his muzzle skyward and let loose a boisterous howl. I, too, raised my head to join him, Ivory's voice strong and clear to warn anyone away who would bring harm to our mate.

Despite the fear racing in my mind, and the thoughts of Amarok and the Trials, my heart was light. My wolf and I were one, and Conri and I were one.

Afterword

Thank you for reading the first book of the Luna Sage series, Scarlet. If you enjoyed it, please leave a review on Goodreads, Storygraph, or anywhere books are sold.

If you want to hear how Scarlet earned her name check out this free prequel, The Legend of Scarlet.

Book Two, Ivory, will be released mid 2023. If you are interested in keeping up with the progress, please follow me on TikTok, Instagram, or Facebook.

If you want sneak peaks, sign up for my newsletter, and join my private Facebook group.

If you want to read more while you wait for Ivory, check out the rest of my books.

For easy access to all my links scan my Linktr.ee QR code.

Acknowledgments

As with all my stories, my main influence and inspiration is my papaw. Wait…I write dark romance, why am I crediting my grandfather? My papaw was my childhood babysitter, and he fueled my imagination. We would sit for hours, just telling stories. As a tribute to him (he passed away when I was in junior high school), I write him into every story. Kassy's Saba is my Saba.

This story was a closely guarded secret, as it shows my darker side, so very few who actually know me have read this.

This story has gone through so much growth since I brought it to the light of day two years ago. The first person to help me shape and mold it is my friend Morgan Perryman. Thank you for all your support and work to bring this story to life and keeping me from losing my mind.

Rachelle Anne Wright is one of the few to have already read books one and two in their most raw forms, and I want to thank her for encouraging me to keep at it.

My family might not know exactly what goes into writing a book or how much mental bandwidth I have poured into this and all my other book babies, but they are still very supportive.

I also want to thank all my beta readers on betareader.io for the fantastic feedback and the love they've shown to Kassy and Conri (and maybe Wolfe). Megan, Anna, Rachel, J.L. Cross, Eliza, this book wouldn't be anywhere without you.

To my critique partners, Liahona, Marissa, Amanda, and Julia, even though you didn't read this story, you've helped me brainstorm my way out of the dark corners and helped me with cover art and generally kept me sane…well, sane-ish.

Of course, this book wouldn't see the light of day without my editor and coach, Maria Secoy & Erin Canning. Thank you for the support and advice.

And finally my friend Liahona for proofreading and beating the "feels" out of this book!

www.ingramcontent.com/pod-product-compliance
Lightning Source LLC
Chambersburg PA
CBHW030816020726
47499CB00006B/1945